Junebug

JUNEBUG

A NOVEL

WILSON
EDWARD REED, PhD

NEW YORK

LONDON • NASHVILLE • MELBOURNE • VANCOUVER

JUNEBUG

A Novel

Published in New York, New York, by Morgan James Publishing. Morgan James is a trademark of Morgan James, LLC. www.MorganJamesPublishing.com

Publisher's Note: This novel is a work of fiction. Names, characters, places, and incidents are either products of the author's imagination or used fictitiously. All characters are fictional, and any similarity to people living or dead is purely coincidental.

Scripture taken from THE HOLY BIBLE, NEW INTERNATIONAL VERSION ®. Copyright©

1973, 1978, 1984, 2011 by Biblica, Inc.™. Used by permission of Zondervan

Proudly distributed by Publishers Group West®

A **FREE** ebook edition is available for you or a friend with the purchase of this print book.

CLEARLY SIGN YOUR NAME ABOVE

Instructions to claim your free ebook edition:
1. Visit MorganJamesBOGO.com
2. Sign your name CLEARLY in the space above
3. Complete the form and submit a photo of this entire page
4. You or your friend can download the ebook to your preferred device

ISBN 9781631959349 paperback
ISBN 9781636981246 ebook
Library of Congress Control Number:
2023930427

Cover and Interior Design by:
Chris Treccani
www.3dogcreative.net

Morgan James is a proud partner of Habitat for Humanity Peninsula and Greater Williamsburg. Partners in building since 2006.

Get involved today! Visit: www.morgan-james-publishing.com/giving-back

To my mother, Willie B. Reed,
and the women who raised me.

I was leaving the South
To fling myself into the unknown . . .
I was taking a part of the South
To transplant in alien soil,
To see if I could grow differently,
If I could drink of new and cool rains,
Bend in strange winds,
Respond to the warmth of other suns
And, perhaps, to bloom.

RICHARD WRIGHT

———

There is no greater agony than bearing an untold story.

MAYA ANGELOU

———

Go back to the past to fetch the best for the future.

SANKOFA

———

REDWOOD, MISSISSIPPI

1956

1

THE BUS

Mama told me if I walked up to the road and stood here, the bus would come get me. But it ain't here yet, and I'm starting to worry. What if the bus driver forgets all about me, and I miss my first day of first grade? I feel all jumpy inside, like I've got a belly full of grasshoppers.

I know I'm supposed to get on the little yellow bus. The big yellow bus takes the white kids to their school. The big yellow bus is shiny and new, and the little yellow bus is old and rickety, but Mama says we're lucky to have a bus at all. Some places, the colored kids have to walk to school, even if it's real far away, and the big bus full of white kids rolls right past them and splashes mud on them. The white kids holler out the window and call them bad names.

I hear it. The bus!

It pulls up right in front of me and slows to a stop. Now I feel excited and scared instead of worried. The grasshoppers in my belly are turning somersaults.

I climb onto the bus. Mr. Johnson from church is the driver. He says, "Good morning," and I say it back, but it comes out soft and shy.

"Junebug!"

I look to see where the voice is coming from. It's my friend, Robert. He lives close, and we play all the time. He's got a big smile on his face and pats the seat next to him. I smile back and go sit beside him.

Riding the bus is fun. Me and Robert look out the window. We pass by fields of cotton where people are already out picking before the sun gets too hot. We pass the church. After a few more minutes, we pass the white school in Redwood, which is big and made of red brick and has an American flag flying from a flagpole. There's a concrete playground with a basketball goal and swings.

White kids are already going inside the building, wearing their new, store-bought school clothes.

We go a ways further to get to Kings, where the colored school is. My school. It has an American flag like the white school, but the schoolyard is just plain dirt. I've seen the school before, but looking at it now, it seems bigger, like I won't be able to find my way around in it. The grasshoppers have started jumping again!

Me and Robert get off the bus with the other kids. I'm wearing my one new outfit that Mama bought on layaway. Some of the other colored kids are wearing hand-me-downs from big brothers and sisters, but the clothes are clean and so are their faces and hands.

As soon as we get inside, a lady in a green dress says, "First graders, follow me!" She takes us to a room with a big blackboard and rows of desks. "Everyone take a seat, please," she says. Saying *please* is polite, and I can tell she is a polite lady. I take a seat next to Robert.

"Good morning, little birds," the lady in the green dress says. "I am Miss Taylor, and we are going to learn a lot this year."

Miss Taylor doesn't waste any time! She starts writing the ABCs on the board right away. I already know my letters, but I don't answer when she asks questions because I feel too shy. What if I get something wrong?

———

"What do you think was the best part?" Robert asks on the bus ride home.

"Recess was the best part!" I say, laughing. Me and a bunch of boys played ball in the schoolyard while the girls jumped rope.

"Lunch was the best part!" Robert says, laughing too.

Lunch was good. At home, we don't eat in the middle of the day, and sometimes, it feels like a real long time between breakfast and supper.

Really, I liked the learning stuff best, but I don't tell Robert that.

My little sisters, Bernice and Dorothy, are in the yard making mud pies when I get home.

"You wanna make mud pies with me, Junebug?" Dorothy asks.

"I don't know. I'm in school now. I might be too big to make mud pies."

Mama is hanging clothes on the clothesline. She hears me and laughs. "You're never too old to make mud pies. I'd be out there making 'em myself if I didn't have so much work to do around here."

Mama works hard. She has a job cleaning and cooking in a white lady's house, and then she comes home and cooks and cleans here too. She says that, even though it's a lot smaller, our little shotgun house is harder to keep clean than the white lady's house because the white lady has running water.

"You need me to fetch you some water so you can start supper before Daddy gets home?" I ask. Fetching water is one of my chores.

"That'd be real nice, Junebug," Mama says. She has a pretty smile. "Did you do your best in school today?"

"It was the first day, so there wasn't that much to do," I say.

"Well, you should still do your best," Mama says, hanging one of Dorothy's dresses on the clothesline. "You only get out of it what you put into it."

REDWOOD, MISSISSIPPI

—————

1961

2

JIM CROW

It's PE class. Me and my friends, Wardell, Robert, and Coot and the other fifth-grade boys, are playing basketball while our PE teacher, Mr. Hart, yells out directions at us. Over at the white school, they've got a gymnasium and a paved basketball court; we ain't got nothing but a dirt yard. But we've got a goal, and Mr. Hart says we don't have to have all that fancy stuff. If you've got a goal, that's good enough.

Back when we were in first and second grade and too little to play basketball much, we used to play this game of tag that Wardell called "Jim Crow." The kid who was "it" chased all the other kids and yelled "Jim Crow's gonna get you!" and if he tagged you, you had to scream and fall down and carry on like he had got you good. But then it was your turn to be *it* and chase the other kids.

When I was that age, I thought Jim Crow was like somebody in the scary stories kids are always telling—like the Boogeyman or Ol' Raw Hide and Bloody Bones. One of those monsters that was supposed to like to eat little kids.

But now that I'm older, I know Jim Crow is worse than any monster anybody could make up.

Jim Crow is the reason we don't have new books and a gymnasium at our school, like the white kids. Jim Crow is why my daddy can't get a steady, good-paying job and why the only job Mama can get is cleaning white women's houses. Jim Crow is the reason we can't eat at the diner and can only sit in the balcony at the Palace movie theatre. Jim Crow is not like the tag game where he knocks you down, but you get right back up again, and then it's your turn. Jim Crow makes things for colored folks so that we get knocked down again and again, and it's never our turn.

"Not so rough, boys!" Mr. Hart yells at Robert and Wardell as they struggle for the basketball.

Robert is one of those people who takes games real serious and plays to win. He must not hear Mr. Hart because he shoves Wardell and takes the ball. Wardell falls with his hands and knees in the dirt.

"Robert Wilson, you're out of the game!" Mr. Hart yells. "Get over here and take your punishment."

Robert grits his teeth because he knows what's coming. We all do. Mr. Hart tells him to get a switch—"and not a little ol' piddly switch either"— from the schoolyard tree. Mr. Hart has so many kids pick switches from that tree it's a wonder it has any branches left.

All us boys watch Robert get his six licks. He stares straight ahead with his jaw clenched. Everybody watching has felt that sting before, so we know it hurts. We also know the only thing that makes it worse is crying in front of your friends. Robert makes it through without crying.

By the time we're on the school bus, we're all laughing about Robert and the licking he got—even Wardell and Robert, who are good friends again now that there's no ball to fight over.

—————

"Robert got a licking at school today," I say. Me and Bernice and Dorothy and Mama and Daddy are all sitting at the table eating beans and cornbread.

"Who gave it to him?" Daddy asks, sopping his cornbread in the bean juice.

"Mr. Hart in PE," I say.

"I bet he did," Daddy says, laughing. "I think Clarence Hart gives more lickings than any other teacher at that school."

"What did he get a licking for?" Bernice asks.

"He was fighting with Wardell over a ball and shoved him," I say, then stuff my mouth with cornbread.

"Boys," Bernice says and rolls her eyes like she's an expert on them or something.

Mama laughs. "Well, boys fight each other, and girls bad-mouth each other. I don't know which one's worse." She gives Daddy a look. He gets in fights sometimes when he goes out on the weekend and gets drunk. Sometimes he'll come home bloody and bruised, and she'll have to patch him up with gauze and iodine.

"Sticks and stones may break my bones, but words will never hurt me," Dorothy says. I reckon it's something Mama Sally or somebody taught her.

"I don't know about that," Daddy says. "Some words hurt. I was man enough to fight for this country, and I still get called 'boy' by every white man who sees me on the street. That's a word that don't feel so good."

———————

Every night after Mama and my sisters clear the table, I sit there and do my homework while Mama washes the dishes. Sometimes, Daddy comes in and talks to her while she works. They always talk real soft, and I guess they think I'm not paying attention because I've got my nose stuck in a book. My sisters always ask me how come I study so much, and I say what my teacher says: education is the one thing nobody can ever take away from you. I love my family, but I have dreams and goals I know they don't understand.

Tonight, I hear Daddy say to Mama, "Did you hear about what happened last night over in Yazoo County?"

Mama nods. "Crying shame."

"I heard there wasn't much left of him when they got done with him," Daddy says under his breath.

Mama shakes her head. "His poor mama."

I know Mama and Daddy don't think I'm listening and don't think I'd know what they're talking about even if I was. And it's true that I don't know exactly who they're talking about, but I don't have to know who he was to understand what happened to him.

Jim Crow got him.

3

COON HUNTING

"You be careful with that gun, son," Daddy says. "Don't go pointing it at nothing you don't mean to shoot."

"I promise I'll be careful, Daddy," I say.

Daddy taught me how to shoot and clean a rifle when I turned ten, but this is the first time he's let me take it out. Me and Robert and Wardell are going coon hunting.

"Are you sure this is a good idea?" Mama asks Daddy. They're sitting at the kitchen table drinking coffee and listening to blues music on the radio station that comes in from Memphis.

"I was out in the woods hunting squirrels and rabbits when I was younger than him," Daddy says. "Hunting's a good way for a boy to learn how to be a man."

Mama laughs, but she sounds nervous. "Hunting's a good way for a boy to shoot his dang foot off."

There's a loud knock on the door.

"They're here!" I say. "Bye!"

I run out onto the porch. Rob and Wardell are waiting for me, each of them with a rifle slung over their shoulder. Rob's carrying a lantern, and Wardell's got a helmet with a light on it that makes him look like a coal miner. They're both smiling and joking around and looking as excited as I feel.

I go out in the woods all the time, sometimes by myself and sometimes with them. But we've never gone coon hunting before, and we've never gone into the woods at night. This feels like an adventure.

"You ready to get us a coon, Junebug?" Rob says.

"I'm ready," I say. I sling the gun over my shoulder. I feel tough and brave, like the cowboys we see when we go to the movies. I wish I was riding a horse, but I don't guess you need a horse to go coon hunting.

We walk toward the woods. The moon is bright, but it's still awful dark.

"We've got to stay together so nobody gets lost," Wardell says.

"I couldn't get lost in these woods if I tried," I say. "I know these woods as good as I know the path from my back door to the outhouse."

Rob and Wardell laugh.

The woods at night are full of music. Owls hooting, crickets chirping, frogs singing. Once we get deep into the woods, it's a lot darker because the trees are so close together, not much moonlight shines through. If it wasn't for Rob's and Wardell's lights, I couldn't see my hand in front of me. The deeper we get into the woods, the darker it gets.

"I hope there ain't no snakes out here," Rob says.

"No," Wardell says. "It's nighttime. All the snakes have gone to bed."

This makes me picture a snake snuggled up under a quilt in a special, extra-long snake bed, which makes me laugh.

"Wait!" Rob says. "Look over there!"

I follow Rob's pointing finger. It's hard to see in the darkness, but up in a tree a few feet away, there's definitely an animal. I can't make out much about it except that its snout is long, and its tail is naked and pink.

"There's you a coon!" Robert says in a whisper. "Go ahead and shoot it!"

I've seen raccoons before, and if this is a raccoon, it's a sorry excuse for one. Where's the mask and the fluffy, ringed tail? "That don't look like no coon I've ever seen," I say.

"Well," Rob says, "that's on account of it being a different kind of raccoon. That there's what you call a French raccoon. Right, Wardell?"

"That's right," Wardell says. "A French raccoon makes for some good eating. That's why they like it over there in France where the food's all fancy. You'd better go ahead and shoot it before it gets away."

I take the gun off my shoulder, raise it, and aim it. As I do, I understand something about myself: I don't really want to kill anything. But I'm no good with a gun, and it's just a one-shot rifle anyway, so all I'll probably do is shoot the tree and scare the critter off.

I pull the trigger. I can't believe it when the French raccoon falls out of the tree like a brick.

"You did it!" Rob says, clapping me on the back.

"In one shot!" Wardell says. "Here, I've got a sack you can put it in."

Rob and Wardell are so happy and proud that I feel happy and proud too. Handling the dead animal and putting it in the sack makes my stomach feel queasy, but if I'm going to be a hunter, I have to get used to these things.

We walk back through the woods with me carrying the gun in one hand and the sack in the other.

"Your mama and daddy are gonna be so proud of you!" Wardell says when we get back to my porch.

"Y'all wanna come in, and we can show it to 'em?" I say.

"No, man, we'd better get on," Rob says. Rob and Wardell live near each other on the plantation.

I'm just as happy to show off my kill by myself. After all, I was the one who shot it. Daddy said hunting was a good way for a boy to become a man. I guess that means I'm a man now.

The house is dark when I go inside, carrying the sack. Mama and Daddy are already in bed, but news this good can't wait. I shake my daddy's shoulder. "Daddy, Daddy! Wake up and see what I've got."

Daddy opens his eyes and yawns. "Did you get a coon, son?"

"I sure did," I say. I reach inside the sack. "But it ain't just an ordinary raccoon. It's a French raccoon!" I pull the critter out of the sack by its naked tail.

Daddy sits up in the bed and scoots away from the dead animal. "I don't know what in the Sam Hill a French raccoon is, but I know that ain't one!"

Mama is awake now too. "Is that a dead possum?" she says. "Junebug, that's nasty!"

Daddy starts to laugh. "Those boys made a fool out of you, Junebug. Get that nasty thing out of the house!" He shakes his head and laughs some more. "A French raccoon."

I stuff the possum back in the bag and take it outside. I walk out to the woods and leave it there where it belongs. I feel bad that it died for nothing. I wish I hadn't listened to my friends' voices telling me to shoot when there was a voice inside me telling me not to.

Rob and Wardell got me good. But I know I can't stay mad at them for long.

4

CHURCH

"Let me see those fingernails, boy!" Mama says. She has on her Sunday best dress, blue with pink flowers. The ribbon on her hat matches the flowers.

"Aw, Mama, I scrubbed 'em when I had my bath last night!" All the kids take turns having a bath on Saturday night. Mama heats up water on the cookstove and pours it into a big metal tub.

"Well, then, let me see 'em," Mama says.

I stretch out my hands, and she frowns at them. "Go over to the washbasin and scrub 'em again," she says.

I frown, too, but I know there's no point in arguing. There's clean, and then there's *Sunday* clean.

When we walk to church, it's like a parade: Daddy in the front in his dark suit and tie, Mama beside him in her pretty hat, my sisters in their best dresses, and me in an ironed shirt and pants and shoes that pinch my feet. It makes me think of that song we sing in church sometimes, "When the Saints Go Marching In."

The church is at the ball ground out by the woods. Behind the church is a colored graveyard. Most of the graves have regular stones with names on them, but some of the graves are so old they're just unmarked rocks. I wonder if there's anybody still alive that remembers who's buried there.

13

I always think the ladies going into church look so pretty, with their dresses and hats all the colors of the rainbow. Mama Sally, my grandma, spots us right in front of the church and opens up her arms for whichever one of us can get to her for a hug first. Her hair is steel gray, and she's wearing a dress and a hat the color of peach ice cream.

I get there for the first hug.

"Look at how handsome you are!" Mama Sally says, looking at me with both of her hands on my shoulders. "Now, you're coming over to my house for dinner after church, right?"

"Yes, ma'am," I say. Sunday dinner at Mama Sally's is the best and biggest meal of the week.

She smiles. "One of my hens met her maker this morning. I hope you're saving room for some fried chicken."

"I've always got room for your fried chicken," I say. My mouth waters just thinking about it.

Mama Sally always says that Mr. Reagan, our Sunday School teacher, has "the patience of Job." Us kids can get silly, especially us boys, but he never yells or gets mad. And somehow, he always manages to teach us a Bible verse and tell us a story and lead us in singing a song before it's time to leave class and go to the big church.

One reason I like church is that I get to see Betty Lou. Today, she has her hair in plaits tied with pink ribbons that match her pink dress. Her eyes are the same rich brown as a bar of Hershey's chocolate, and her eyelashes are long and fluttery. It's not just that she's pretty, though. Some pretty girls are real mean. But Betty Lou's nice.

One day, I passed her a note in school telling her I like her, and she wrote back and said she likes me too.

I don't know what gets into me, but when we're leaving Sunday school to go to the big church, I lean over and whisper to her, "Meet me out back at noon."

She whispers "okay" and gives me this shy smile.

I melt like butter on a hot biscuit.

Once everybody has settled down on the long wooden benches in church, Mrs. Simpson starts in on the upright piano. She plays real loud and peppy, like she's trying to get everybody excited. As soon as she plays a few notes, everybody knows what song it is: "He's Got the Whole World in His Hands." I can't even remember a time I didn't know this song.

Everybody stands up and sings about how God is holding everybody in His hands—the little bitty babies, all the brothers and sisters. It's about how God loves everybody, no matter whether they're big or little or rich or poor or colored or white. It's a song that makes you feel taken care of, like one of Mama Sally's hugs. And everybody singing it together, swaying back and forth, clapping their hands, feels good too.

"That was just beautiful, brothers and sisters," Brother Charles says. He's wearing his usual dark suit, and his bald head is shining in the sunlight pouring through the window behind him. "It's beautiful when we raise our voices in praise together—when we, as the poet said, 'lift every voice and sing.'"

"Amen," say a couple of voices in the congregation.

"And the Lord really does hold all of us in His hands, praise God," Brother Charles says, starting to pace like he always does once he gets wound up. "He holds us up even when there are those on earth who want to hold us down."

"That's the God's truth," an old man in the second row says.

"But He holds us up. He lifts us up to the heavens!" Brother Charles says. "And brothers and sisters, we've got to hold each other up too. We've got to remember to share an encouraging word, a smile, with our brothers and sisters. Right now, I want you to turn around and greet your neighbor. I want to see handshaking! I want to see back patting! I want to see hugging!"

The closer it gets to noon, the more I feel all nervous and quivery. Once it's time, I look at Betty Lou across the room. She gives me a little nod, then gets up and excuses herself past her brothers and sisters. It's not unusual for people to leave church for a couple of minutes, then come back. The service is long, and sometimes nature calls.

But Betty Lou and me aren't going to the bathroom, even though I mouth the word "bathroom" to Mama when I squeeze past her. It's a wonder I don't get struck down right there for lying in church.

Betty Lou's waiting for me behind the church, all shy smiles. "We can't stay gone too long, or both of us will get in trouble," she says.

I nod. If I'm gone too long, I know Mama will give me The Look when I come back. Later, I'll get a talking-to, at best, a spanking at worst. "Betty Lou," I say, "I want to . . . I want to . . ." I know what I want, but I can't seem to say it or do it either.

"Do you want to kiss me, Junebug?" Betty Lou says. Her eyes are already closing, her pretty lips puckering like in the movies.

I lean forward and touch her lips with mine. Her lips are as soft as a pillow, a cloud. I feel like I'm floating on a cloud as I kiss her.

When I pull away from her, she's smiling. I smile too.

"We'd better get back," she says.

After I sit back down in church, I start worrying. Did the dead people in the graveyard see us kiss? Is God mad at us for kissing outside of His house? I know all the grown-ups would say we were way too young to be kissing. They'd call me a mannish boy and Betty Lou a fast woman.

At Sunday dinner, Mama Sally heaps my plate high with fried chicken, macaroni and cheese, collard greens, yams, and cornbread. It's all delicious, but while I'm eating, something is eating me. I look at my family—Mama, Daddy, Mama Sally, Dorothy, Bernice, and my aunts, uncles, and cousins—and feel the pain of my terrible secret. I'm not a saint. I'm a sinner. My family can't see it, but God sees everything.

5

MOVIES

"We'll meet you at this door when the show's over," Mama says. She has on her second-best dress, the yellow one. She wears it whenever we come into town. "Now y'all be on your best behavior," she says.

"Yes, ma'am," Robert and Wardell and me say in a chorus. We're standing beside the Palace Theatre in downtown Vicksburg. I have that tingly, excited feeling I always get when I'm going to the movies. It's *Tarzan* today, my favorite.

"Now, I'd better not hear about y'all throwing popcorn down on the white people," Mama says.

We say "yes, ma'am" again, but we can't look at each other, or we'll laugh. Maybe we've thrown popcorn down at the white people one or two times before.

White folks go through the front doors of the theatre, under the big lighted marquee. Colored folks have to go in through the side door, I reckon because the white folks don't want to look at us. After we go in the side door, we go up the stairs so we can sit in the colored balcony. There's always an usher by the door to the balcony selling bags of popcorn. Downstairs at the concession stand, where we're not allowed to go, they have candy and Coke too.

17

But I still love popcorn, and I love movies no matter where we have to sit.

"I hear Tarzan wrassles an alligator in this one," Wardell says.

"He wouldn't wrassle no alligator," Rob says. "He'd wrassle a crocodile cuz that's what they've got in Africa."

"Crocodiles are way meaner than alligators," I say. I remember reading that somewhere. Alligators are slow and sleepy, unless you bother them, but crocodiles will jump right out and eat you up.

"I wouldn't wrassle neither one of them," Wardell says. "But Tarzan would, and then he'd say, 'See you later, alligator . . . after 'while, crocodile!'"

We all laugh, but then the lights go down, and it's time for the movie. I always feel a little thrill when they turn the lights off and the big red velvet curtain opens.

There's never a dull moment in a *Tarzan* movie. I love seeing all the animals. This one has elephants and lions and monkeys. Tarzan does wrestle a crocodile, holding its jaws open with his muscular arms. There are African natives, too, but Daddy told me the first time he took me to see a *Tarzan* movie that they're not real. "Shoot, son," he said, "those ain't Africans. They're just actors. The people making the movie put them in grass skirts and stuck bones in their hair and told them to jump around, holding spears and saying, 'Ooga-booga, ooga-booga.' Real Africans is just regular colored folks like us."

I didn't know whether to be glad or disappointed.

At a part of the movie where there's no Tarzan or animals on screen, just people talking, Wardell nudges me. I watch him take a small handful of popcorn and pitch it over the balcony. Rob does the same, and finally, I do too. For some reason, throwing popcorn off the balcony and onto the heads of the white people is the funniest thing ever.

We watch white ladies brush popcorn out of their hairdos. Some white people look up at us and say, "Knock it off."

We don't knock it off. But I do want to be careful not to waste all my popcorn. I want to eat most of it; it's so crunchy and salty and good.

Finally, one white high school boy with close-shaved hair stands up, faces the balcony, and yells, "Quit it!" But he doesn't just yell *quit it*. He also calls us the name that Mama says is the ugliest name there is.

We stop throwing popcorn and laughing.

The movie's still good though. Tarzan is back on screen, saving a white man and a white woman who are sinking in quicksand. He rescues them just before their heads go under.

It's funny. The *Tarzan* movies are set in the African jungle, but there sure are a lot of white people in them. None of the main stories are ever about colored people, even though Africa's supposed to be full of colored people. How come Tarzan, the king of the jungle, is a white man? I don't spend too much time thinking on this, though. Instead, I grab myself a big handful of popcorn. It goes in my mouth, not over the balcony.

REDWOOD, MISSISSIPPI

1963

6

CHANGE

When I get home from school, Mama Sally and Aunt Sis are sitting on the front porch, snapping beans. For the past month or so, they've come over a couple times a week and cooked and cleaned so that when Mama comes home from work, she's got a nice house and supper ready.

I must have a funny look on my face when I walk up on the porch because Aunt Sis says, "What's the matter, Junebug? Ain't you glad to see us?"

"Yes, ma'am," I say. "It's just . . . I've been wondering how come y'all are coming out here and helping Mama so much."

"Well, there's gratitude for you," Aunt Sis says, but she's got a smile on her face. Aunt Sis is sour and sweet at the same time, vinegar and sugar all rolled into one.

"No, he don't mean nothing bad by that," Mama Sally says. "Kids just notice when somethin's different." She looks at me real close. "Junebug, your mama's tired. Women work hard—colored women, especially—and sometimes they get tired and need a little extra help."

Now that I think about it, Mama has seemed to have less energy lately. She's gotten skinnier, too. Her dresses fit looser. She doesn't dance to the radio when she washes the dishes anymore, and sometimes after supper, she falls asleep sitting on the couch. I think about something Mama always used to joke about when she came home from work: "If I clean that white woman's house all day, who's gonna clean *my* house?" I guess Mama Sally and Aunt Sis are the answer to that question. "I'm glad you're helping her," I say.

Mama Sally smiles. "You be sure to help her, too, Junebug. Ask her if there's any more chores you can do around the house."

"Yes, ma'am," I say, but to be honest, I don't know much about housework. Most of what I do to help is outdoor stuff, like chopping wood or tending the garden. "Is there anything I can do to help y'all right now?"

"Well, you can stay away from the beans," Aunt Sis says. "Menfolk always leave too many strings on 'em."

"But you could go fetch some water so we can get the beans to cooking," Mama Sally says.

"I reckon that's a job he can handle." Aunt Sis smiles at me so I know she's teasing.

When I bring the water into the house, I see that Bernice and Dorothy have been put to work, too, sweeping and wiping down the kitchen. Once I set down the bucket, I ask, "Hey, have y'all noticed that Mama seems tired-er lately?"

Dorothy stops working and says, "Sometimes ladies get real tired when they're gonna have a baby—that's all I'm saying."

This is news to me. I know where babies come from, but not how a woman feels when she's going to have one. "They do?" I say.

"Uh-huh," Dorothy says, picking up the wiping rag again.

"If Mama was gonna have a baby, why wouldn't she tell us?" I say.

Bernice and Dorothy share a look. I can tell this is something they've been talking about. "You know how grownups are," Bernice said. "Always keeping secrets from us kids."

"Hmm," I say because I can't find any more words. What would we do with a baby? Our little house is already so full of people; I don't know where we'd put it. In a dresser drawer?

Mama Sally and Aunt Sis come in, so we stop talking. Kids can keep secrets from grownups, too.

It's just a feeling I have, but I don't think Bernice and Dorothy are right about Mama expecting another baby. Something about her is different, though, and it makes our whole family feel different. There's a change in the air, and whatever it is, I don't like it.

7

MAMA

"Junebug, your mama wants you to take her a glass of water," Mama Sally says.

"Yes, ma'am," I say. Lately Mama's been missing work and staying in bed all day. Except for the days when Daddy's drunk too much moonshine the night before, nobody in our house stays in bed into the day. Mama Sally and Aunt Sis are here just about all the time now, cooking and cleaning and helping out.

When I carry the glass of water into the bedroom, Mama says, "Close the door, Junebug." Her voice sounds weak and scratchy.

I close the door and take her the water. She takes one tiny sip, then sets the glass on the bedside table. "Sit here on the bed with me, Junebug," she says.

I sit on the edge of the bed. I don't think a glass of water was the real reason Mama asked me to come in here.

"I'm real proud of you, Junebug," she says.

"Thank you," I say. The way the light from the window is hitting Mama's face, I can see how much weight she's lost. Her face used to be fuller, but now, her cheekbones jut out as sharp as blades. Her color's not good either—there's a grayness to her skin instead of the usual warm brown.

"You're so smart, and you do so good in school. Also, you're a nice boy—good to your sisters and good to your friends." She smiles a little. "And I can't hardly believe you're thirteen. You're so big. You're not my baby boy anymore, except in my heart."

"Aw, Mama," I say, embarrassed.

"Now you need to listen to me good, Junebug. I ain't one to make speeches, but I've got some things I have to tell you."

"Yes, ma'am."

Mama takes my hand and holds it. I can feel the shape of the bones in her fingers. "Son, I ain't gonna be here for very much longer."

"Ain't gonna be where? What are you talking about?" I ask, even though the tears welling up in my eyes mean I know good and well what she's talking about.

"Ain't gonna be in this world much longer," Mama says. "For a long time the doctor was telling me I was just tired or I wasn't getting enough vitamins, but then I saw another doctor, one in Vicksburg, and he told me it was cancer."

Cancer. A word so bad people didn't even like to say it. "Can't he . . . cut it out or something?"

Mama shakes her head. "No, it's spread too much. Your Mama Sally and Aunt Sissy are praying for a miracle, and I reckon you can pray for one too. But miracles don't happen every day, Junebug, and so there's some things I want you to promise me."

I nod my head because I'm crying too much to say anything.

"With me gone, you're gonna have to be the man of the house. You're gonna have to look after your sisters. Make sure they get enough to eat and go to school every day and to church on Sundays."

"I'm only thirteen. I can't be the man of anything. Won't Daddy be the man of the house?" I'm sobbing as I talk. Definitely not manly.

Mama gives me a sad smile. "Junebug, you know what your daddy's like. He means well most of the time, but he ain't steady, and he don't always make the best choices." She takes a deep breath like she's trying to calm herself. "I need to tell you something, Junebug, but you've got to promise you won't tell nobody else about it, and I mean nobody."

"I promise."

"Your daddy . . . he's got another family down the road."

I can't make sense of what she's saying. It's like she's not even talking English. "I don't understand."

"He's got another woman and a couple of children by her, Junebug. He kept it from me for years, till I finally got wise to it. If you go up the road to where you catch the school bus and take a right, there's a little shack painted blue with a dirt yard. That's where she lives—and where he lives part of the time. I'm telling you this so you'll know why you have to be man of this house. Your daddy can't be man of this house if he's man of another house too."

It's too much. I can't believe it. I won't believe it. "That's got to be a mistake. You've got to be wrong. Wrong about Daddy, wrong about the cancer, wrong about everything!"

Mama looks at me with sad eyes. "I wish I was, honey."

"But you are!" I say, standing up. I can't stay in this room anymore and listen to things that hurt too much to be true. "I'll prove you wrong. You'll see! You'll see!"

I tear out of the bedroom and past Mama Sally and Aunt Sis.

"Should I go after him?" Aunt Sis says.

"Nah, he needs to be by himself a while, let it all soak in," Mama Sally says.

I run out of our yard and up the road to where I catch the school bus, then I take a right like Mama said. After another minute of running, I see it. A wooden shack that's painted the color Mama Sally calls "haint blue." There's a little boy a few years younger than me in the dirt yard, playing some kind of made-up game with a stick and a tin can. None of this means anything, I tell myself. Maybe because Mama doesn't feel good, it's made her confused in her head.

I stop running and walk closer to the shack. "Hey!" I call to the boy. "Can you come here a minute?"

The boy runs up to the side of the road where I'm standing. I'm about to ask him if he knows a man named Reed, but as soon as I look at him up close, I don't have to ask. His eyes are just like mine.

"What?" he says.

"Nothing," I answer and take off running into the woods.

I run till I'm out of breath, then I sit down on a rock and let the tears come again.

REDWOOD, MISSISSIPPI

1964

8

FUNERAL

"Who can find a virtuous woman? For her price is above rubies," Brother Charles reads out of his battered black Bible. "Brothers and sisters, we have come here today to remember a virtuous woman."

The casket, covered in flowers, is in front of the pulpit. I look down at my shoes to keep from looking at it. Mama Sally says it's not really my mama in that box, that Mama's soul has already flown up to Jesus. But I can't stand to think of the mouth that used to smile at me, the arms that used to hug me, the feet that used to dance to the songs on the radio, all shut up in that box.

We all go to Mama Sally's after the funeral. Brother Charles too. There's lots of crying and hugging. Daddy goes outside with some of the men, and I know they're going out behind the barn to drink moonshine. I guess drinking makes this day easier for him. But I don't think Daddy deserves to have things easier. Ever since Mama told me about his other woman and kids, I've been mad at him. I've not said anything about it, but I think he knows I know.

There's a huge amount of food in the house. When there's a death in the family, it feels like food magically appears out of nowhere. There's ham and fried chicken and potato salad and sweet potato pie and a whole coconut cake. All stuff I love. I'm usually the boy who's always hungry, but today, I don't feel like eating anything.

I'm too filled up with sadness to feel hungry.

Robert and Wardell come up to me, looking uncomfortable in their church clothes. But there's something else uncomfortable about them, too. When you're a kid yourself, what do you say to a kid whose mom just died, who's going through the worst thing another kid can imagine?

"Hey," Wardell says, giving me an awkward pat on the shoulder. "I'm sorry about your mama."

"Thanks," I say. I know if I look him in the eyes, I'll start crying.

"I feel so bad about your mama too," Robert says. "But me feeling bad ain't enough to make you feel better. I don't know what the right thing to say is."

"There's not a right thing to say," I answer. "Thanks for being here."

I'm glad my friends are here with me. But I've never felt so alone.

———

Mama's been gone two weeks, but it seems like there are bits and pieces of her all over the house. At least once a day, Bernice or Dorothy or me will pick up a dishrag she used or the tomato-shaped pincushion she liked and start crying.

Mama Sally and Aunt Sis bring us groceries and things we can eat out of for a few days, like big pots of beans or vegetable soup. Daddy isn't home much. When he's not at work, I guess he's at his other home or maybe off drinking somewhere. I see what Mama meant when she said I'd have to be the man of the house.

Bernice and Dorothy are learning how to be the women of the house. They try to keep things clean. They try to cook. They don't always succeed, but they try. They make fried eggs with broken yolks and burnt fried baloney sandwiches. Whatever they make, I eat because I know they're trying their best.

I'm trying too. With no money coming in from Mama's job, things are tight, so I'm trying to do odd jobs and cut grass to help out as much as I can. Today, I'm answering an ad I saw in the newspaper for somebody who can weed a garden and mow grass. It's a long walk to the address. When I finally get there, I see it's a nice white, two-story house with a lot of yard to mow and a big garden around back. It looks like a lot of work, but hopefully more work means better money.

I climb up onto the porch. It's real comfortable-looking, with a porch swing and wicker furniture with soft-looking cushions. But I know I'm not here to make myself comfortable.

I ring the doorbell. After a couple of minutes, a heavyset white man answers the door. He's dressed like he's about to play golf. "What are you doing here?" he asks, real hateful.

"I'm here about the yard work, sir," I say, being just as polite as I can.

"Huh," he said. "I didn't expect a colored kid."

"Does it matter?" I ask, hoping it doesn't sound like I have a smart mouth. What I really want to say is, *I'm here to cut your grass, not date your daughter.*

"It matters," the man says. "But I don't suppose it matters so much I won't let you do the work. Come on, and I'll show you where the lawn mower's at." He takes me to the toolshed around back and shows me a shiny, brand-new lawn mower. "Now, I like the grass cut real close, like what you see on a golf course."

"Yes, sir," I say. What is it with white people and golf?

"And after you mow, you can go ahead and weed the garden. You ever weeded a garden before?"

"Yes, sir," I say. "My mama"—I almost say *keeps*, then stop myself—"*kept* a garden."

"All right then," he says. "Don't bother me till you're done."

I say "yes, sir" one more time for good measure, then start up the mower. As I work, I notice a white boy my age in the house's driveway shooting a ball at a real basketball hoop. It would be fun, I think, to have a basketball hoop right at your house. I figure the boy who gets to play while I work must be the man's son.

The mowing takes a long time, and when I'm finished, I'm thirsty. But I know better than to ring the doorbell and ask for a glass of water. If nobody was around, I might risk a quick drink from the garden hose, but the boy's still outside practicing his basketball. I move on to the garden, squatting down to pull out the tiny weeds growing between the tomato plants. I think about picking a juicy red sun-warmed tomato and how good it would feel to bite into it and let the juice run down my chin. But I figure the man would look at me helping myself to a tomato the same as if I broke into his house and stole his TV and his wife's jewelry.

As I get to the end of a row, I feel somebody behind me. I look up and see the man standing over me.

"You're not doing a bad job, boy," he says.

"Thank you, sir."

"You know what?" he says, pointing at a plant in front of me that has little red cones hanging from its branches. "You ought to try one of them. They're juicy and sweet, like candy."

My mouth is so dry that anything juicy is tempting. "Thanks," I say, pulling off one of the little red cones and standing up.

When I take a bite, the juice that floods my mouth is like liquid fire. My eyes and nose stream like I'm a human waterfall. I'm coughing and sputtering and can't catch my breath. When I look through my weeping eyes and see the man, he's bent double, laughing. It's like I'm the funniest thing he's ever seen.

"That's a cayenne pepper, boy!" he says, between belly laughs. "It'll set your little black butt on fire!"

I run past him to the garden hose and drink all I can. It helps some but not much. I'm burning from the pepper, but I'm burning mad too. Why did this stranger feel like it was okay to play a mean prank like that on me? I bet he wouldn't do it to his own son or any of his son's white friends. To him, me being colored means I'm just something for him to laugh at. He wouldn't even care if he knew that I make good grades in school or that I just lost my mama. To him, I'm no different than a dog you tease by pretending you're going to give it a treat before you yank it away.

When I finish the weeding, he gives me a five-dollar bill. We need the money, but part of me wants to throw it back in his face. I don't, though. I stick it in my pocket, say, "Thank you, sir," and walk away.

9

MISS MAY

Daddy brings the woman into our house and introduces her like she's the Queen of England. "Stand up, stand up," he says to Bernice, Dorothy, and me.

We stand face-to-face with the woman and the three boys standing beside her. One's pretty close to my age, and then there's the one I saw before who's maybe three years younger than me. The third one's pretty little. The oldest boy is lighter skinned with green eyes, but the two younger ones are darker and look just like Daddy.

As for the woman, she's nowhere near as pretty as Mama. She's wearing a housecoat and slippers, even though she's left her own house, and she's the kind of skinny that looks mean. She's meeting us for the first time, but she can't seem to spare a smile.

"This here's Miss May," Daddy says, "and her boys, Curtis, James, and Will." He points out the boys from oldest to youngest. "They're gonna be staying with us for a while."

I feel a knot form in the pit of my stomach. Out in the country, *a while* can mean anything from three days to forever.

"How long is a while?" Dorothy asks, like she's reading my mind.

"Well," Daddy says, sounding stern, "I reckon a while is however long they want to stay. Y'all's job is to make them feel welcome."

"Where's everybody gonna sleep?" Dorothy asks. It's a good question. Eight people in a two-bedroom shotgun house is a tight squeeze.

"Well," Daddy said, grinning like he's embarrassed, "we figure for now, Curtis can sleep on the couch, and we'll make pallets for James and Will on the living room floor."

"For now," Miss May emphasized, looking at her boys.

I notice Daddy didn't say where Miss May was gonna sleep, but I think I have a pretty good idea.

"Yeah, later we're gonna build another room onto the house," Daddy says. "Then we can have a room for the girls and a room for the boys."

It seems to me that in this plan, the boys are getting the short end of the stick. The two girls get a room all to themselves while I have to cram in with three boys I just met. But it doesn't matter, anyway. I recognize Daddy's tone as what Mama always called *talking a good game* . . . when he goes on about plans he has for something he'll never have the time or money to do.

Finally, I say what's on my mind. "So, this situation is permanent?"

"I sure hope so," Daddy says, smiling at Miss May. When she smiles back at him, I notice for the first time that there's not a tooth in her head.

"You're not our mama," I blurt out.

"Honey, I never said I was," Miss May says. It's like she's trying to sound sweet, but she's not fooling me. She'd be a lot happier if Bernice and Dorothy and me weren't in the picture.

"She ain't your mama, but she's still gonna be the lady of this house, so you need to treat her with better manners than y'all are treating her with right now. And you have to mind what she says the same way you have to mind me."

Dorothy and Bernice and me look at each other. We can say a lot without saying a word. Right now, what we're saying is something along the lines of, *We thought things were as bad as they could be, but now they're worse.*

There's a knock on the door, then a call of "Helloooo!" before the door opens. It's how Mama Sally always enters the house. She's carrying a big pot of something that smells delicious, and Aunt Sis is right behind her with a round pan wrapped in foil, which is probably a pie.

"Hey, Mama," Daddy says, sounding nervous.

Mama Sally looks over at Miss May and the boys, and her smile fades. "Why, Wilson, I didn't know you had company." She glances at the stack of bags and boxes Miss May and her kids have brought into the house. Mama Sally is smart. She knows this isn't just a visit.

Daddy looks really nervous now. His forehead has broken out in sweat, and he can't look Mama Sally in the eye. "Let me introduce you," he says.

"Oh, I know who it is," Mama Sally says. She sets the pot on the stove. "Junebug, would you come outside with me and Aunt Sis and help us with something for a minute?"

"Yes, ma'am," I say, happy for the chance to escape.

As soon as we're out the door and on the porch, Aunt Sis says, "Can you even believe him shacking up with that woman before his wife is even cold in the ground—"

"Sissy," Mama Sally says and makes the "shh" sign with her finger over her lips.

"I don't care if they hear me. I don't care if the whole county hears me. I'm mad enough to spit nails!" Aunt Sis says. She's really getting wound up.

"I'm mad too," Mama Sally says, "but I don't want nobody to say nothing that'll upset the children worse than they already are." She puts her hands on my shoulders and looks me in the face. "Junebug, I'm sorry your daddy's acting the fool. I think he's lonesome with your mama gone and can't stand the thought of not having a woman to take care of him. What I'm praying for is that it won't take him long living with her to figure out that she ain't a thing like your mama, and then he'll send her on her way. You should pray for that too."

"Yes, ma'am," I say, my voice cracking like I'm about to cry.

"And in the meantime, you take care of your sisters and yourself," Mama Sally says. "Me and Sis will come around and look in on y'all every few days, but our door is always open. If you ever need us, promise you'll come on over."

"I promise." It seems like Mama Sally always shows up when you need her, like a fairy godmother in a story.

Aunt Sis has been pacing the porch, but now she stops and looks at me. "And if you want to know the reason you ain't got a mama no more, all you have to do is go back in that house and look at that woman." Aunt Sis's eyes flash with anger. "That woman put the hoodoo on your mama!"

"Sissy," Mama Sally says again, shushing her.

Mama always said that Christians should know better than to believe in superstitions like hoodoo. And I do know better. But I also know that my mama died of cancer, and because she did, now Miss May has the man she wants and a two-bedroom house instead of a one-room shack. Miss May may not have killed Mama, but she's sure glad Mama's dead.

10

NEW FAMILY

"She looks like a witch," Bernice says.

"She *is* a witch," Dorothy says, and they both giggle.

I think of what Aunt Sis said about Miss May putting the hoodoo on Mama. "No, she ain't a witch," I say. We're out in the garden, picking the beans and tomatoes that Miss May would be content to let rot on the vine. "But she *is* a lazy heifer."

Bernice and Dorothy giggle even harder.

I was trying to be funny, but I was telling the truth, too. Before she got sick, Mama was always doing something—working at her paying job, cooking and cleaning at home. Even when she sat down at the end of the day and listened to the radio, she'd still be fixing a hole in a sock or doing some other little bit of sewing. Her hands were never idle.

Here's what Miss May does: she sits on the couch and watches her "stories" all day on the TV Daddy bought her. And she dips snuff and spits the disgusting brown juice in a rusty old coffee can. When Daddy comes home, she gets up to fix supper, but it's not a real cooked supper like Mama would fix. It's fried baloney or government cheese on light bread or pork 'n beans cold out of the can. The only real cooked food we get is what Mama Sally and Aunt Sis bring. And whatever food there is, you can bet Miss May makes sure that her kids get the best and biggest portions of it before me and Bernice and Dorothy get any. It'll always be Dorothy or Bernice or me who gets the heel off the loaf of light bread, not one of Miss May's kids.

While my sisters and me are working in the garden, Miss May's sons are out in the yard playing stickball and having a good ol' time. They never have to do any chores, but me, Dorothy, and Bernice keep up with our chores like always because we know Mama would've wanted it that way.

"Well," Dorothy says, looking down at the sack of beans we've picked. "I reckon we've got a mess of beans. We might as well snap them and cook them for supper tonight."

"I'm sure her highness in there won't mind if we take over the cooking tonight," Bernice says.

I pick up the sack of beans and tomatoes. "It'll be good to have a hot meal that ain't fried baloney," I say.

I help Bernice and Dorothy snap the beans and they put them on to cook with a little piece of fatback like Mama used to do. There are a few potatoes in the potato bin, so I wash them and throw them in to cook with the beans while they mix up some cornbread.

When Daddy comes home, he says, "Something smells good," and kisses Miss May on the cheek. She doesn't say it's my sisters doing the cooking and that she hasn't been up off the couch all afternoon.

"Bernice and Dorothy are cooking tonight," I say. I'm not going to let Miss May take credit for my sisters' work.

"Well, that's good," Daddy says. He gives Miss May a squeeze on the shoulder. "They're giving you a little break, huh?"

I don't say anything because a whipping from Daddy's about the last thing I want, but I can't help thinking, *A break from what?*

At supper, we have the green beans with potatoes, sliced tomatoes, and cornbread. It's not as good as Mama would've made, but it's still good.

"These beans is a little stringy," Miss May says.

"It's not like you're gonna get the strings caught between your teeth," Dorothy says under her breath, and her and Bernice and me can't help but laugh. Miss May's sons look daggers at us.

"Y'all mind your manners," Daddy says. "In this house, children treat adults with respect."

"Yessir, Daddy," we all say.

But it's hard to treat Miss May with respect because she's never shown the slightest interest in whether we live or die. She cares about that TV set way more than she cares about us. And it's not as easy to respect Daddy as it used to be. How could he possibly think that couch-sitting, snuff-spitting Miss May is a proper replacement for Mama?

VICKSBURG, MISSISSIPPI

———

1965

11

THE WORLD

My world is bigger.

There isn't a colored high school in Redwood, so once I finished eighth grade, Daddy decided we should move to Vicksburg. "You get yourself an education, maybe you'll have an easier time getting somewhere than I did," he said.

It's funny. Sometimes it seems like Daddy doesn't care about you at all, but then he surprises you.

I've been a country boy all my life, but I guess I'm a town boy now. It's exciting, but it's also scary the way things that are new are always scary.

Today, I get on a yellow school bus full of kids I've never seen in my life. I've got on a new pair of pants and a new shirt from the Sears-Roebuck catalog, but a lot of these kids are dressed a lot nicer than me. I guess town kids just look fancier. I find an empty seat and settle in for a silent bus ride. I miss Robert and Wardell and the joking around we used to do on the bus in Redwood.

When I see the school, my jaw drops. It's huge. And not just that—it's new. Rosa A. Temple High School is built in the modern style, all sharp angles and brick and glass. And it sits on a huge piece of land with a football field and a track. I've never seen anything like it. Well, I've never seen anything like it meant for colored people. We're used to having to settle for the old, the broken-down, the second best, but this is a building white kids would be proud to call their school.

The school being so nice makes me happy, but it makes me nervous, too, like maybe I don't deserve to be here. But Daddy moved us to Vicksburg for my education, and I hear Mama's voice in my head saying, "You can do it, Junebug." And so I take a deep breath and walk through the school's double doors.

It's so bright inside; I blink a few times like somebody coming out of a coal mine into the light. The morning sun pours through the many windows, and the white walls and tile floors are so clean, they shine. It's hard to believe this is a place where I'm welcome, where I'm supposed to be. But I know it is because all the other kids are colored too. The difference is they all seem to know each other and know where they're going, and I'm alone and lost.

I must look as lost as I feel because an older lady wearing a green plaid dress and pearl earrings says, "Are you new?"

"Yes, ma'am," I say. "Very."

She laughs kindly. "It's a big building, isn't it? What's your name, dear?"

I almost say my family nickname since it's all anybody in Redwood called me, but I remember I have to be official, so I say, "Wilson Reed, Junior."

"I'm Miss Evans. I teach history. Are you a freshman, Wilson?"

"Yes, ma'am."

"Well, then, let me walk you to your homeroom."

As Miss Evans escorts me down the hallway, she points out useful landmarks like the cafeteria and the library, helping me get my bearings and feel a little more at ease. The classroom she takes me to is full of other kids whose last name starts with *R*. It's a sea of strangers, so I sit down in the first seat I see.

The tallest woman I've ever seen walks through the door. She is wearing a light gray blouse and skirt, and her hair is arranged in a roll at the nape of her neck. *Elegant* is the word that pops into my head. "Good morning, scholars!" she says. "Stand up, please, for the Pledge of Allegiance." We say the pledge just like we did in grade school, then the teacher says, "Now I've got copies of all of your schedules, but it's going to take a little while for me to hand them out. So listen for your name to be called and try to keep the noise down to a dull roar."

After the bell rings, I hold my schedule like a security blanket and go to my first class, English. I'm surprised to see that my homeroom teacher is also my English teacher. "Good morning, scholars!" she says again. "I'm Miss Clayton, and I'll be your guide for this class. I say guide instead of teacher because we're going to be exploring together . . . exploring the power of written expression. For example, take a few moments and read the poem by Mr. Langston Hughes that I have copied onto the board."

I read the white words chalked on the blackboard:

I, too, sing America.
I am the darker brother.
They send me to eat in the kitchen
When company comes,
But I laugh,
And eat well,
And grow strong.
Tomorrow,
I'll be at the table
When company comes.
Nobody'll dare
Say to me,
"Eat in the kitchen,"
Then.
Besides,
They'll see how beautiful I am
And be ashamed—
I, too, am America.

I read Mr. Hughes's words again and again. I feel like they are singing in my blood. I've never read anything like them. "It's true," I say out loud without meaning to.

"What's true?" Miss Clayton says, putting me on the spot.

I don't really want to be the first person to speak in class, but I also don't want to clam up when the teacher asks me a direct question. "What the poem says," I say. "About colored people being America too. Like my daddy—he fought overseas, but when he came back here, nothing had changed or was better. He always says colored folks love America, but America don't love them back."

"Yes, that's an excellent example. What was your name, please?"

"Wilson Reed, Junior, ma'am."

"That was a fine comment, Mr. Reed. 'Colored folks love America, but America doesn't love them back.' That's exactly what Mr. Hughes is pointing out in the poem while saying that we're as much America as anybody else. Do any other scholars have comments to make?"

I feel a warm glow in my chest. Most of the warmth comes from Langston Hughes's words, but some of it's from Miss Clayton, too, for making me feel like what I said was worth something.

The cafeteria is so big and crowded with strangers that I almost don't go inside. But I'm supposed to get free lunch, and I'm always hungry, so I'm not going to pass up the opportunity to eat. I get a tray and get in line and am surprised to be served meat, two vegetables, a roll, and some canned peaches. I grab a little carton of milk and look across the tables, trying to find a spot to eat my feast without having to beg strangers for a place to sit. Finally, I find one long table with four kids sitting on one end. I choose the opposite, empty end and start shoveling in my food. It's not as good as Mama Sally's cooking, but it's lots better than anything Miss May puts on the table.

A lanky, sharp-dressed kid carrying a tray stops at my table. "Hey, you've got first period English, right?" he says.

"Yeah," I say. "Miss Clayton."

"That was good what you said in class," he says. "Mind if I sit here?"

"Be my guest," I say.

"I'm Mike. I don't know anybody here yet," he says, sitting down across from me. "My family just moved from Jackson."

"Big city, huh?" I say. "My name's Wilson, but my friends call me Junebug. I don't know anybody, either, because my family just moved from Redwood, which I bet you ain't even heard of."

"Can't say I have, Junebug," Mike says, smiling. "You're as country as cornbread, huh?"

"I guess so," I say, feeling embarrassed.

"That's all right," Mike says. "It'd be a boring world if everybody was the same. Like one thing I've noticed,"—he looks around the cafeteria—"is these kids who only hang out with kids the same color as them. Like over there, you've got a table full of light-skinned kids, and over there, you've got a table full of dark-skinned kids. What's that about? It makes no difference to white folks how light or dark we are—we all have to put up with the same Jim Crow jive, you know?"

"You've got that right," I say. "City or country, light or dark, it's all the same."

"Hey," Mike says, "what bus do you ride?"

"Number five," I say.

He smiles. "Me too. I'll save you a seat."

———

The house we're renting in town has one thing in common with our old house in the country: it's too small for so many people. We're still tripping over each other and getting on each other's nerves, and the kids are still divided into two teams: Mama's kids and Miss May's kids. And there's no doubt which team Miss May is rooting for.

We're all crowded around the kitchen table, eating fried baloney and pork 'n beans Miss May hasn't even bothered to heat up. One thing that hasn't changed for Miss May going from country life to town life is the way she spends her time. Every day, she's still parked in front of the TV, watching her stories and dipping her snuff.

"How was school, Junebug?" Daddy asks.

"It was good," I say. "At first I was nervous because the building was so big—"

"Seems to me," Miss May says, talking over me, "that a near-grown boy living in town ought to see about getting a job."

"Well," Daddy says, "it's important for Junebug to finish high school—"

"I ain't saying he should drop out of school," Miss May says. "But there ain't no reason why he couldn't get a job after school carrying out groceries at the Jitney Jungle, help out the family a little."

"Well, he might do that after he gets settled in school," Daddy says. "But we've got to think about the future—"

Miss May rolls her eyes. "It's hard to think about the future when you ain't got enough right now."

And Daddy and Miss May start going around and around, and then supper's over, and I never even got to answer Daddy's question.

The new house has one bedroom more than the old one, which means that now there's Daddy and Miss May's room and a girls' room and a boys' room. Dorothy and Bernice are lucky. Me, I have to bunk in with Miss May's three sons who poke and smack at each other like The Three Stooges until they finally fall asleep. After that, they snore and pass gas all night.

But tonight, they don't even bother me because I keep thinking of the poem we read in Miss Clayton's class. I love the part when it says, "They'll see how beautiful I am and be ashamed." I close my eyes and think of a country where colored people feel beautiful and the white people feel ashamed of the way they've treated them. It's something to dream about.

VICKSBURG, MISSISSIPPI

———

1966

12

HOME

Home is bad. Daddy comes home drunk pretty often, and he and Miss May argue for hours. And then there's the fussing between Miss May's kids and my sisters and me. Most days, I get up early and get out of the house before anybody else wakes up. That way, I can start my day fresh without having to deal with anybody else's hangover, anger, or bad mood.

Today, since it's more than an hour till the bus runs, I walk over to the colored YMCA on Jackson Street. Until some kids at school told me about it, I didn't know such a thing existed in the world. It's become a second, better home for me. The big red-brick building has a swimming pool and an indoor basketball court, so you can play even when it's raining. When I walk in this morning, Henry at the front desk says, "Good morning, Junebug. How's tricks?"

"Tricky," I say, giving my first smile of the day. "Good morning to you too."

"There's fresh coffee and doughnuts in the lounge if you want some," Henry says.

Having snuck out of the house without breakfast (which is a trade-off I'm willing to make), I head to the lounge. Mr. Johnson, an old man who works for the city, and Mr. Simmons, a younger man who works in an office, are enjoying their coffee and doughnuts and reading the newspaper. Both of them rent rooms at the Y.

"Hey there, Junebug. Come and get you one of these doughnuts," Mr. Johnson says. He's already dressed in his coveralls for work. Soon, he'll be sweeping the streets and emptying trash cans.

"Don't mind if I do," I say. I grab a doughnut and a paper cup of coffee. I'm not a big coffee drinker, but it tastes pretty good if you put in enough cream and sugar. I proceed to pour in enough of both to make it light and sweet.

"Having some coffee in your sugar there, Junebug?" Mr. Simmons says, laughing. He's wearing his suit and tie for work. He sells insurance to colored families.

"I thought I might," I say, laughing. "Mind if I join you?"

"You're always welcome at our table," Mr. Simmons says. "How are things at home?"

During my time hanging out at the Y, I've talked to Mr. Simmons and Mr. Johnson a little about the problems in my family. They're good listeners, not the kind of people who jump in and give you advice before they've heard everything you have to say. "Pretty rough," I say. "Daddy's drinking too much. Him and Miss May fight a lot. Miss May's kids fight with Dorothy and Bernice. I try to stay out of it, but I've got to defend my sisters, you know?"

Mr. Johnson and Mr. Simmons nod.

"With all the yelling, it gets so loud it's hard for me to study. I've taken to going to the library after school and staying till it closes." But the colored library closes at six, so that still gives me plenty of time to have to put up with the craziness at home.

"Well, the most important thing is for you to keep up with your studies," Mr. Johnson says, dunking his doughnut into his coffee. "Gotta get your diploma. That's your ticket to better things."

"That's right," Mr. Simmons says. "Things are changing, and you want to be a part of them. Look here." He holds out the newspaper and points to an article about the Voting Rights Act President Johnson signed. "You know what this means? No more poll taxes. No more tests colored people have to pass or they can't vote. We get to choose our own representation in the government."

"We'll see," Mr. Johnson says. "We live in Mississippi, remember? It's gonna take some time for this state to practice what the government's preaching."

"That's true," Mr. Simmons says. "There's some ignorant white people in this state."

"We're counting on your generation to make things better, Junebug," Mr. Johnson says.

"No pressure," Mr. Simmons says, smiling.

After two doughnuts and a cup of coffee, I decide to use up some of the sugar and caffeine playing basketball in the gym. A shy young man named Gregory who also lives at the Y is there, and we take turns shooting hoops—not talking, just playing. He's a lot better than I am, but I have fun anyway. I never claim to be a great athlete.

After about fifteen minutes, I wave bye to Gregory and go to take advantage of the Y's world-class men's room. I had never had a real hot shower before I started coming to the Y. The house in Redwood had no running water, and our house in town has running water but only a small bathtub, which Miss May wants us to use just once a week so we don't run up the water bill.

But I don't have to pay the Y's water bill, so just about every morning before school I take a hot shower, so hot that it almost scalds me clean. The warmth relaxes the tension in my shoulders and my neck, all the tension I carry around with me because of what's going on at home. By the time I get out, dress, and brush my teeth, I feel like a whole new person.

When I walk into the school now, it's not like it was back when I didn't know anybody or know where anything was. Instead, when I walk in, lots of people—students and teachers—say, "Hey, Junebug" or "Good morning, Mr. Reed." I'm not a football hero or one of the popular light-skinned fraternity brothers, but teachers know me as a serious student, and kids know me as someone who's nice to everybody and easy to get along with. I've made a place for myself at Rosa A. Temple.

Sometimes I think Vicksburg is a city of temples. Rosa A. Temple is a temple for the mind, and the Jackson Street Y is a temple for the body. My favorite temple, though, is the colored public library. It is my personal temple of the mind, where I can read anything that interests me. Today, after school, I'm returning *The Weary Blues*, a collection of Langston Hughes poems I borrowed two weeks ago. I take the book to Mrs. House, the librarian who is kind of like how Mama would've been if she'd been able to get an education.

Mrs. House accepts the book with a smile. "*The Weary Blues*," she says. "I think we all know what those feel like sometimes. Did you have a favorite poem in here, Junebug?"

"I loved them all. I think 'Mother to Son' made me cry the most, though."

"It's a beautiful poem," Mrs. House says. "So what are you going to read next?"

It's always an exciting question. "I want to read something else by a Negro author." I've been starting to notice that writers like Hughes said "Negro" instead of colored.

"Well, let's see what we can find for you." Mrs. House walks out from behind the desk. She's wearing a pretty powder-pink dress and pearls. "Now, does it have to be poetry, or might you prefer a novel this time?"

"Let's try a novel," I say. I love the way I can disappear into a story, how I can read and read and the rest of the world falls away. Nobody else in my family seems to know this pleasure.

Mrs. House scans the shelves and finally pulls out a book. The books in the colored library are all secondhand, but Mrs. House makes sure they're in good reading condition. "This one, I think. Though it's really an autobiography that's written like a novel."

I take the book from her and look at the cover. "*Black Boy* by Richard Wright," I read.

"It is tremendous," Mrs. House says. "It might even change your life." She smiles. "But you've got to finish your homework before you start reading it!"

It takes me an hour to do my homework, and then I start reading *Black Boy*. I've always loved reading, but I've never read anything that feels so close to my life. Like me, Richard Wright grew up poor in Mississippi with a mama who was sick and a daddy who often felt like a stranger. Like me, he knew the horrors of Jim Crow and what it's like to grow up in a place where people think you don't even have the right to exist. Like me, he was more sensitive than the other kids around him and lost himself in books. I'm so deep into reading that Mrs. House has to pat me on the shoulder and tell me the library is closing.

"You missed supper," Miss May says as soon as I walk in the door.

"I'm sorry," I say. "I was at the library."

"Wasting your time with your nose in a book instead of finding an honest-paying job," Miss May says, looking at me like I'm the world's biggest disappointment. "I gave your supper to Curtis. He was here, and he wanted seconds."

"I don't care," I say, even though I am hungry. The next words spill out of my mouth before I have a chance to think about them. "It probably wasn't worth eating, anyway." The yellow smears on the plates Bernice and Dorothy are clearing show that supper was Miss May's rubbery scrambled eggs.

Daddy rises to his feet. "What did you say to her?"

I've already realized my mistake. "I'm sorry, Miss May."

She frowns and crosses her arms.

Daddy says, "I didn't tell you to apologize. I told you to repeat what you said to her." His voice is as hard as steel.

I know I'm doomed. I take a deep breath. "I said the food she fixed probably wasn't worth eating anyway, but I'm sorry I said it."

"Sorry isn't good enough, boy! I thought I raised you to *honor* your mother and father."

I stand up straight and look Daddy in the eye. "I try to honor you, Daddy. And I do honor my mother. I honor her every day. But that woman,"—I nod in Miss May's direction—"is not my mother! She's like a buzzard that was circling overhead when Mama died, waiting to see what she could pick up."

Miss May gasps and stomps out of the room. Daddy is already taking off his belt. He bends me over the back of an armchair and whips with the belt. Dorothy and Bernice cover their eyes, but Miss May's kids laugh like it's the funniest thing they've ever seen.

It's strange. Used to, I'd cry when Daddy whipped me. But now, I've got no more tears to shed. It's almost like I'm on the outside, watching myself get a whipping. Daddy's trying to hurt me, but I won't give him the satisfaction.

When he's worn himself out, he lets me go, and I run to my bed, open up *Black Boy*, and pick up reading where I left off. In the story, Richard gets into an argument with his Uncle Tom, who criticizes everything Richard does. When his uncle says he wants to be an example to Richard, Richard says, "You're not an example to me . . . you're a warning."

This is exactly how I feel about Daddy. I can't turn into him, so full of anger and resentment and pain that he has to drink away because he can't put it into words. If I stay here, I'll be as eaten up with anger as he is. Mama told me to be the man of the house, but Bernice and Dorothy are old enough to take care of themselves. If I'm going to be the man I want to become, I can't stay.

13

MOVING OUT

This morning I get up before everybody else to leave the house like normal. But this time, I take more than just my schoolbag and my toothbrush. I take a paper grocery sack with a few clean shirts, another pair of pants, socks, and underwear. I pocket the little bit of money Mama Sally slipped me when we moved to Vicksburg. Part of me wants to wake up Dorothy and Bernice and tell them what I'm doing, but I know if I do, they'll try to stop me, and if they cry and beg me to stay, I might not be strong enough to do what I have to do. I'll tell them later, once it's already too late for me to turn back.

When I walk out the front door and close it behind me, more feelings than I can name wash over me all at once. I feel free and relieved and scared and many other things all at the same time.

Henry's in his usual station at the front desk of the Y. "Hey, Junebug, how goes it?" he asks.

"It goes," I say. I approach the desk. "Henry, I'd like to rent a room here."

Henry raises an eyebrow. "You're awful young to be renting a room at the Y. Don't you live at home with your folks?"

"I did," I say. "But it's gotten to be a real bad scene." I'm covered in welts from where Daddy whipped me last night, and I'm willing to show them to Henry if I have to. "I need a place to stay. I've got money, and I'm gonna get a job."

Henry looks at me. I must look desperate because he counts out the money and says, "This is enough for three nights." He hands me a paper form and a pen. "When you fill this out, say you're eighteen."

I'm so happy I could hug him, but I don't. "Thanks, Henry."

My room at the Y is small and clean, with a single bed, a chest of drawers, a desk and chair where I can study, and a window with a view of an alley. It feels strange to even say "my room" because I've never had a room of my own before. I sit down on the bed and look around. *Mine.* I think, *I've never had something that was just mine.* I'm free to do whatever I want here. I can keep the light on at night and read as long as I want. I can lay around in my underwear, and nobody can stop me. I can go downstairs and play basketball or swim.

But if I'm going to live this way, I've got to have money, so today after school, I've got to pound the pavement to find a job. I laugh, thinking about how Miss May wanted me to get a job so she could get her hands on the money. Any money I get is going into my hands only, unless I need to help out Dorothy or Bernice.

After school, I get off the bus two stops early so I can catch my sisters on their walk home.

"Junebug, what are you doing here?" Bernice says.

"I've got to tell y'all something," I say. "I've split."

"Split what? Your pants?" Dorothy says, laughing.

"No," I say, looking around as if there might be spies watching us. "I've left home. Not that *that* house feels much like home with that woman in it. I got me a room at the Y."

Dorothy and Bernice's mouths are wide *O*s of shock.

"What'll we tell Daddy?" Dorothy asks.

"Tell him I'm safe, but I can't live there anymore."

Bernice's eyes sparkle with tears. "I'll . . . I'll miss you, Junebug."

"I'll miss y'all too," I say, trying not to cry myself. "But I can't stay there anymore. All the anger, it's eating me up inside. I'll still see y'all, though. And I'm at the Y if you need anything."

I give both my sisters a quick hug and then walk toward downtown in search of a job.

I see a sign in the Bluebird Diner's window that says, "Dishwasher wanted." When I go in and ask about it, a white waitress takes one look at me and says, "Oh, we already hired somebody for that. We just forgot to take the sign out of the window." I thank her anyway and leave. As I do so, I notice she doesn't make any move to take the sign out of the window.

The other restaurant downtown, the D&W, has a sign saying, "Busboy wanted." When I go inside, I get the exact same runaround from the manager, saying the position has already been filled and that—surprise!—they forgot to take the sign out of the window. Here's what they really mean: We don't want to hire somebody colored.

The new Kentucky Fried Chicken on the outskirts of town has a "Now Hiring" sign out front. I'm starting to feel discouraged, but I've got to find something, so I go inside. The smell of frying chicken hits my nose and makes my mouth water. "Can I help you?" a freckle-faced, brown-haired white girl behind the counter asks. She doesn't sound as suspicious of me as the other white people I've talked to today.

"Yes, please," I say, putting on my politest *talking-to-a-white-person* voice. "I saw the *Now Hiring* sign and wanted to ask about a job."

"Oh, you'll want to talk to the owner, then," she says. "Hold on, and I'll go get him."

"Thank you," I say. For a second, I picture the girl returning with the actual Colonel Sanders, with his goatee and white suit and cane. I almost crack myself up but hold it in because I want to make a good impression.

The white man who comes out is middle-aged and has enough of a belly that it looks like he helps himself to a fair amount of the Colonel's chicken. "I'm Frankie Stevens," he says. "And you are?" His tone isn't friendly or unfriendly, just matter-of-fact.

"Wilson Reed, Junior, sir," I say.

"And how many hours a week can you work, boy?"

Even with the unwanted "boy," I take this question as a good sign. At least he's not saying they've already hired somebody for the position. "Well, I'm still in school, so I'd have to work evenings during the week, but I can work anytime on the weekend."

He nods as if this is satisfactory. "Well, let's get you an application."

I fill out the one-page application, remembering to list the Y as my permanent address. I put down Miss Clayton from school and Mrs. House at the library as references. When I hand Mr. Stevens the paper, he glances at it and nods. "All right," he says. "We can start you at a dollar twenty-five an hour. You'll have to work in the kitchen. Only white folks out front. We'll start you out with washing cookware, cleaning the bathrooms, mopping up, that kind of thing. But if you do a good job, we'll train you to cook."

"Does this mean I'm hired?" I ask.

He nods. "Can you be here tomorrow at four-thirty?"

"Yes, sir," I say.

"You get a free meal every shift," Mr. Stevens says. "I don't care how much you eat so long as you work hard."

"That's great," I say. Between morning coffee and doughnuts at the Y, free lunch at school, and a free meal at work, I'm going to eat better than I ever did at home.

"I thought you'd be happy about the free fried chicken," Mr. Stevens says, chuckling.

I know what he's getting at, the idea that colored people are crazy for chicken. I've never really understood why this is one of the things white people say. I mean, doesn't everybody like fried chicken? But like so many other colored people so many other times who have needed money, I ignore his racist comment and say "yes, sir" and "thank you."

"Hey, Lisa Jean," Mr. Stevens calls to the girl at the counter. "Why don't you pack up some chicken for Wilson here to take home with him? He's gonna start work here tomorrow."

I sit at my desk in my room at the Y and eat the salty, greasy fried chicken and mashed potatoes and coleslaw. It's *my* food, and I'm eating it in *my* room, and there's nobody here to criticize me or whip me or tell me what to do. And I've found a way I can support myself and stay in school, too. I'll try to slip money to Dorothy and Bernice when I can, with the condition that Miss May can't lay her hands on it.

I think Mama would be proud of me. I enjoy my peaceful, silent meal and feel very grown up.

————

VICKSBURG, MISSISSIPPI

1967

14

JIM CROW CHICKEN

My nickname for KFC is JCC, which stands for Jim Crow Chicken. Walking into the restaurant is like seeing a miniature version of Jim Crow in action. Mr. Stevens, the white boss, keeps everybody in their place. The white workers are out front, where it's cool and comfortable, wearing their clean uniforms and taking people's money. Smiling at customers is part of their job description, and they get to work a whole shift without breaking a sweat.

In the hot kitchen in the back, where nobody can see us, are the employees Mr. Stevens calls "the colored help." Most shifts, it's Maurice, who's in his early thirties and has been working in restaurants since he was in eighth grade, and Sharon, a young mother who leaves her little girl with her sister while she works. I'm the baby of the group and get told so often. But in a nice way. I like the people I work with. I can't say the same for the person I work for.

Mr. Stevens struts around the restaurant like a peacock, joking around with customers and flirting with the white girls who work the counter, even though he's almost old enough to be their daddy. In the kitchen, he yells at us to work faster and finds fault with everything we do. If there's a crumb on the floor or a splash of grease on the wall, he cusses us out so bad that if Mama Sally heard him, she'd wash his mouth out with soap.

61

Except when he counts money out of the cash registers, I've never seen him do a lick of work.

When I was in school back in Redwood, there was a story in one of our books called "The Elves and the Shoemaker." In the story, after the shoemaker went to sleep at night, elves would come into his workshop and make beautiful shoes. When the shoemaker woke up in the morning, there would be these perfect shoes waiting to be sold. The shoemaker never saw the elves, and he took all the credit and the money for the shoes. The KFC is kind of an "Elves and the Shoemaker" situation, except the invisible elves are in the kitchen frying chicken instead of making shoes.

Today, I'm prepping the mashed potatoes while Maurice is dropping chicken in the fryer.

"It's gonna be a miracle if I make rent this month," Maurice says. He's already sweating from standing over the hot grease.

"But it's payday today," I say.

"Yeah, but there ain't gonna be much money in my paycheck this time around."

"That don't make sense," I say. "You work more than I do." Maurice and Sharon put in around forty hours a week, while I just put in about twenty-five.

Sharon looks up from the pot she's washing and says, "Maurice, you didn't let Mr. Stevens give you an advance on your paycheck again, did you?"

Maurice looks embarrassed. "I didn't have no choice. My car broke down, and I had to have the money to get it fixed. No car means no work means no money."

"Yeah, but taking money from Mr. Stevens means money today but no money tomorrow," Sharon says.

Mr. Stevens's moneylending practices were well known at the KFC. If he knew you were strapped for cash, he'd act all friendly and offer you fifty or even a hundred bucks as an "advance" on your next paycheck. Then he'd take that money out of your next paycheck, plus twenty-five percent interest. This was a trick he only tried with the "colored help" in the kitchen. It wasn't like we weren't wise to it, but like Maurice with his car trouble, when you're poor and you have limited choices, sometimes you make the one that'll see you through today and figure you'll worry about tomorrow when it comes.

"Don't be criticizing me, Sharon, or you won't get none of the barbecue chicken I'm fixing for us today," Maurice says. "I made up some sauce at home, and I figure I'll slather some chicken with it and roast it in the oven."

"Sounds good," I say. All of us get sick of the Colonel's recipe because we've eaten so much of it, so we're forever trying out new ways of cooking chicken for our meal breaks. It's like we've got two restaurants going, one for KFC and one just for ourselves.

On Friday evenings, I always go see my family after work, so I load up all the unsold chicken I'm allowed to take, plus mashed potatoes and coleslaw and rolls. I'm filling up a bucket when Mr. Stevens walks in.

"Oh, it's fried chicken night at Wilson's house," he says. "Everybody's gonna have a good time tonight. You people love you some fried chicken."

"Lots of people love fried chicken," I say. "That's why KFC's such a big business. You see white people in here eating chicken every day, don't you?"

I can feel Maurice's and Sharon's eyes on me. They know that, for Mr. Stevens, what I just said amounts to back talk.

Mr. Stevens gets so close in my face that I can smell the coffee and cigarettes on his breath. "You think you're awful smart, don't you? Reading your books on break and using all them big words. But being book smart won't get you nowhere if you've got a smart mouth."

The anger bubbles up inside me, but I tamp it down for the same reason Maurice took an advance on his paycheck even though he knew it was a bad idea. Mr. Stevens controls the money, and I need money to survive.

———

"The Chicken Man's here," Miss May says when I come in the door. She's taken to calling me Chicken Man like it's my superhero name or something. Probably because bringing chicken to the house is the only thing I do that she considers useful.

"Two buckets full?" Daddy says, taking one of the containers out of my hands. "We're gonna be eating chicken all weekend."

"That was the idea," I say.

Daddy and me get along a lot better when we don't live under the same roof. When I first moved out, he was so mad he wouldn't talk to me for a month. But after a while, he settled down. He finally told me he couldn't judge me, that he'd moved out of his family's house as a teenager too. Plus, I figure not having me at home anymore took some pressure off him because it meant one less mouth to feed.

And now I help feed the family some, too, by stocking their fridge with fried chicken every weekend.

"Did you get me and Dorothy some drumsticks?" Bernice asks.

"I did," I say, "and wings for Miss May and the boys."

"Thanks, Junebug," Bernice says. She and Dorothy set the table, and everybody gathers around and helps themselves to chicken and potatoes and coleslaw and bread. There's so much food that everybody can eat as much as they want, which is a luxury our family rarely has. Even Miss May's boys thank me for bringing supper.

It's a nice visit, and one of the things that makes it nice is knowing that when I'm ready, I can go back to the Y and sleep peacefully in my own room. Visiting the house is much better than living there, especially when I come bearing buckets of chicken and am greeted as Chicken Man, a superhero.

15

A FINE MIND

Richard Wright. Langston Hughes. Zora Neale Hurston. Gwendolyn Brooks. These are writers whose books I've checked out of the colored library. Their words have opened up my mind and heart to what it means to be Black in America. Even though I've never met any of these authors, they are my teachers, my mentors. Their truths feel eternal.

From the newspapers I read every day at the Y, I get the truths of day-to-day life. Because of the newspapers, I know about the March on Selma and the riots in Watts. I know James Meredith marched through Mississippi, and a white man shot him before Meredith had even been marching for two days. Because of the newspapers, I know where the civil rights workers are marching, and I know when the police attack them with clubs and hoses and tear gas. How do Dr. King and his followers remain so calm in the face of such violence and hatred? Could I wait quietly for service at a lunch counter with people throwing slurs and hot coffee at me? Could I sit there and take it, like Dr. King wants us to, or would my anger bubble up so much that I would say or do something to put myself and others in even worse danger?

Most nights, once I've finished with my homework, I sit in the lounge with Mr. Simmons and Mr. Johnson and Gregory and play cards, though we don't take the card game too seriously. Mostly, we use the cards as an excuse to talk about whatever's on our minds. Well, everybody except Gregory. He's the quiet type, but when it comes to games, he plays to win and usually does.

Tonight, as Mr. Johnson deals me in, he says, "So how's things over at the chicken coop?" The chicken coop is his nickname for KFC.

"Not so good for the chickens," I say. "Not so good for the workers either, except for the boss who seems to be doing just fine and dandy."

"That sounds like every job I ever had," Mr. Johnson says.

"Yeah," Mr. Simmons says. He's loosened his tie and rolled up his shirtsleeves. "But times are changing, right? Our people are going to have more opportunities. That's why you young fellas need to prepare for the future. What are you doing to prepare for the future, Gregory?"

Gregory gives a shy smile and says, so softly that I have to lean forward to hear him, "I'm . . . I'm learning how to fix cars. That's how come I moved to Vicksburg. To apprentice with a mechanic."

"That's good!" Mr. Simmons says. "That's real good. How about you, Junebug? What are you doing to prepare for the future?"

It's not a question I've given much thought. I want to stay in school and be the first member of my immediate family to graduate, but I've never imagined what my life will look like after graduation. I guess I spend all of my energy on scraping by in the present, so there's no energy left to plan for the future. "I don't know, Mr. Simmons. I guess I just focus on getting through the day I'm in."

"That's survival, not living, Junebug," Mr. Simmons says. "You need to decide what you want your life to look like. You don't want somebody else deciding that for you."

———————

"Mr. Reed, may I see you for a moment after class?" Miss Clayton asks.

"Yes, ma'am," I say, and then I spend the rest of the period worrying about what I could have done to get in trouble instead of thinking about *Romeo and Juliet* like I'm supposed to be.

I wait till the rest of the class clears out before I approach Miss Clayton's desk. I don't want to be embarrassed in front of my friends.

When Miss Clayton looks up from her papers at me, she smiles. "You look like you're waiting for the judge to read your sentence," she says.

"I . . . I just don't know what I've done, ma'am," I say. For the past hour, I've been racking my brain trying to figure out what offenses I could've committed.

"Well," Miss Clayton says, "what you've done is write an excellent paper. Perhaps the best one in the class."

I think I must have heard her wrong. "I did what?" I say.

"You heard me the first time." She hands me the paper, which she has marked with a red *A plus*.

"Well, thank you," I say, feeling even shyer than I did when I thought I'd done something wrong.

"Thank you for putting such thought into the assignment," Miss Clayton says. She looks at me like she's sizing me up. "Mr. Reed, have you ever thought about college?"

I'm so surprised I laugh. My answer would be the same if somebody asked me, *Have you ever thought about hippopotamuses? Yes, I've thought about them as something that exists, but I've never imagined that they could have anything to do with me.* "Not really," I say.

"Well, you should." She taps me gently on the head with a pencil. "You've got a fine mind inside that skull of yours."

———————

If I have a fine mind, I sure don't need it to work at KFC. By now, I've been working there so long that I can do all my tasks automatically without thinking about them. I've become a robot.

Today, Sharon is worried because her little girl has an earache and needs to go to the doctor. "She's kept me up three nights straight," Sharon says. She does look tired. "I've tried every one of my granny's home remedies, but nothing's working. I hate to have to pay out the money, but I can't have her hurting all the time."

Mr. Stevens seems to have Superman's hearing when it comes to people talking about problems that cost money. He appears in the kitchen and says, "Sorry to hear about your little girl, Sharon. But you've got to get her to a doctor. You can't mess around with ear problems. You don't want her to go deaf, do you?"

Sharon winces a little. I can tell she can't stand to think of something bad happening to her daughter.

"But doctor visits cost money, and medicine costs money," Mr. Stevens says. He reaches into his shirt pocket and pulls out a crisp fifty-dollar bill. "Why don't you let me give you an advance on your check to help out your little girl?"

Sharon looks down at the pot she's washing. "No, thank you," she whispers.

"What was that?" Mr. Stevens says, putting his hand up to his ear.

"I said no, thank you," Sharon says a little louder.

"No, thank you, you don't want to help your little girl?" Mr. Stevens says.

"No, thank you, I don't want an advance on my paycheck," Sharon says.

We all know Mr. Stevens's advances are a trap, but they're still a trap easy to fall into when times are tough.

Mr. Stevens shakes his head and sticks the bill back into his pocket. "Your loss," he says. "Suit yourself. But don't say I never tried to help you." He strides out of the kitchen.

"He almost got you," Maurice says. "I saw you thinking about it."

"Sometimes," Sharon says, "I think that man is the devil."

VICKSBURG, MISSISSIPPI

———

1968

16

NAT TURNER'S REBELLION

The last time I went to the library, Mrs. House reached under her desk and said, "I've got something I've been saving for you." It was a huge, thick biography of Nat Turner, the hero who led a rebellion of his fellow slaves, armed with fence posts and kitchen knives and farm tools. Turner and his rebels managed to kill more than fifty white people before they were caught. The rebellion also had the effect of scaring white slaveholders far and wide. *If this group of slaves rebelled and killed their owners*, they must've thought, *what's keeping mine from doing the same thing to me?* It was like white people suddenly got the memo that maybe Black people didn't enjoy being enslaved.

The powers that be killed Nat Turner, horribly and publicly. Turner was hanged and then his body was stripped of its skin, which was then dried and made into change purses for white people to buy as gruesome souvenirs. His execution was a warning to other possible rebel slaves: *See, this is what will happen to you if you try to fight for your freedom.*

Before his execution, somebody asked Turner if he regretted what he had done. He said, "Was Christ not crucified?" Cool as a cucumber, right till the very end.

I've been reading the Nat Turner book whenever I have a few spare minutes, and I'd drop everything and read it till I finished it if I could. I want to learn my people's history. I want to know our heroes.

I take the book, which is too big to fit in my schoolbag, to KFC so I can read it on my dinner break. Mr. Stevens comes into the kitchen while I'm putting my apron on.

"You know, Wilson, I've been thinking," Mr. Stevens says.

That's a new thing for you, isn't it? I think, but all I say is, "Yes, sir?"

"I've been thinking maybe I shouldn't let you take all that free food for your family on Friday nights." He rubs his chin like he wants to demonstrate how thoughtful he is. "I've been thinking that maybe you've been taking advantage of me."

How could a broke, Black teenager take advantage of a full-grown white businessman? "I'm just taking food that would be thrown out anyway," I say. "How's that taking advantage?"

"See, that's what I mean," Mr. Stevens says. "I let you take home some food, and then all of a sudden, you feel like you've got the right to question me. You feel like you can smart off to me. That's the way it is with you people . . . give you an inch and you'll take a mile."

I glance over at Maurice and Sharon, who are both looking down and silently doing their work. I know they'd help me if they could, but all that'd do is put them in danger of losing the jobs they need to survive.

"I won't take the food anymore," I say. "I'll just throw it away and let it go to waste." *Or I'll take it when you're not looking,* I think. Mama Sally always says that wasting food is a sin.

"I'm not in the business of feeding anybody's family for free," Mr. Stevens says. "I don't get to feed my family for free, so why should I feed yours?" He looks at the shelf behind me, where the Nat Turner book is sitting on top of my schoolbag. "That's an awful big book you got there, boy," he says.

"It's about Nat Turner," I say. "He led a slave rebellion in 1831. He fought for freedom." Even as I say it, I know it's a bad idea to try to give Mr. Stevens a history lesson, but I can't stop myself.

"Fought for freedom, my—," Mr. Stevens curses, curling his lip in disgust. "Sounds to me like he was just another"—he uses the term my Mama said was so bad—"who didn't know his place. I bet he got showed it pretty quick, though." He reaches behind me and snatches my book. "I'll show you what I think of your book smarts." He holds the book up in the air out of my reach.

"Give me back my book, please," I say, grabbing for it but missing.

Mr. Stevens laughs. I'm sure he thinks it's hilarious to see me beg. He waves the book in front of me, then runs out of the kitchen with it. I chase him. He darts into the men's room.

"I'll show you where this book belongs!" he says. He starts tearing out pages. The ripping sound is sickening.

"Please, it's a *library* book," I say.

"Well, they don't need books like this in the library," he says. "I'm doing a public service." He tears off more and more pages, stuffs them in the toilet, and flushes.

"Stop!" I yell. I don't care if there are customers in the dining room who can hear me. I don't care who hears me. I lunge toward Mr. Stevens and tackle him, pinning him down on the bathroom floor. A voice in the back of my brain says, *What are you doing? Get off of that white man.* But a voice from deep inside my belly says, *What do you think he'll do to you if you let him go?*

He manages to twist his arms free and pushes me off him, so I fall backward and land on my butt, bumping the back of my head hard on the bathroom sink.

"Now," he says, standing up and straightening his mussed clothing, "you're gonna unclog that toilet."

I look at the ruined book in the now clogged toilet, at the water that's now spilling out of the bowl and onto the floor. "No," I say. "You made the mess. You clean it up." Mama used to say this to us kids all the time, but it's different when it's a Black kid saying it to a white man.

I march out of the bathroom toward the kitchen.

Mr. Stevens loses his words. He's just making enraged sounds, a growl followed by a roar as he runs toward me.

"Wilson, what in the world is going on—" Sharon says, but then Mr. Stevens answers her question by grabbing my left arm and twisting it behind my back. I use my free arm to elbow him in his soft belly.

He lets go of my other arm, doubles over, and says, "Oof."

"Stop it!" Sharon yells.

But I'm so mad that her words mean nothing. Like an angry bull, I charge at Mr. Stevens and head-butt him in the chest, throwing off his center of gravity and making him land hard on the kitchen floor.

Sharon is chanting, "Stop it, stop it, stop it," like a prayer.

"All right, all right," I hear Maurice saying over Sharon. "We need to settle down now."

But I'm tired of settling. All of my anger—about Mama dying, about Daddy moving in Miss May, about me and other colored people not being treated like citizens in our own country by people like Mr. Stevens—all of it boils up so hard and fast, I'm like a pot that's boiling over. I straddle Mr. Stevens, pinning him down, and look at his bloated, red face. He's mad, but he's scared too.

Scared of me.

I want him to hurt. I want him to feel a fraction of the pain people like him have caused people like me for generations.

But then, suddenly, I'm cold and wet and gasping for breath. I don't understand until I look up and see Sharon holding a dishpan that must've held the water that's now drenching me. "You've got to stop," she says.

I feel two arms pulling me back. I try to shake them off, but they're strong. "All right," Maurice says, "Enough of this. Up you go." Then he looks down and says, "Mr. Stevens, you need a hand up?"

"No," he says, pulling himself up. "I'm all right." He grabs some paper napkins decorated with images of Colonel Sanders and uses them to dab the sweat from his face. He looks at me, shakes his head, and walks out of the kitchen.

"Here, you need to put some ice on the back of your head," Sharon says to me. "You got a bad pump knot coming up back there."

I take the ice pack. "Thank you," I say, not just thanking her for the ice but also for stopping me from doing something that could have easily landed me in jail. "How'd you think to pour water on me, anyway?"

She smiles a little. "Well, when the dogs in Mama's yard start to fighting, I always turn the hose on 'em."

Maurice laughs, and finally I do too. It feels good to let out some of the tension.

"Best thing to do now is get back to work like nothing happened," Maurice said. "Wilson, you gonna come over here and help me make this chicken finger-lickin'?"

I join him at the frying station. I'm moving stiffly, and I know I'll be sore tomorrow. "You know what?" I say. "I bet the chicken recipe isn't even the Colonel's. I bet he stole it from some Black lady who worked for him and took credit for it."

"Wouldn't be the first time, won't be the last," Sharon says.

We all get back to work quietly. As the minutes pass, it feels more and more like the fight with Mr. Stevens didn't even happen, like it was something I dreamed. He stays out of the kitchen for the rest of the shift. I like to think it's because he's humiliated. Sharon was the one who stopped the fight, but it still ended with me on top.

But I'm not fooling myself. I didn't win the fight. That's the thing about Jim Crow. The fix is always in for you to lose.

By the time I get off work and start my walk back to the Y, my head hurts a lot. I'm also worried because I don't know what I'm going to tell Mrs. House about what happened to the book. The truth, I guess. I'll figure out some way to pay the library back later.

I know I put myself in danger tonight—in danger of losing my job, in danger of getting arrested. But at least I didn't lie down and take the abuse. I rebelled. I'm the Nat Turner of the KFC.

The difference is, they didn't have airplanes or Greyhound buses in Nat's day, so he got caught. But I don't have to run on foot. If I can save up enough money, I can jump on a bus or a plane and go so far away, Jim Crow can never find me.

17

A CHOICE

"For goodness' sake, Junebug, what happened to you? You're all stove up, and that's some knot you've got on your head." Mama Sally is looking me over. "Sis, why don't you go fix him a warm compress?"

I'm sitting in Mama Sally's spotless living room. After the fight, she was the person I wanted to talk to. Besides Mama, she's who I trust most in the world.

Aunt Sis brings me a warm washrag and presses it to the bump on my head, which makes me wince. "You better not tell us you walked into a door to get that," Aunt Sis says.

"I got into a fight," I say.

Mama Sally clucks her tongue. "Now, Junebug, what have I told you about fighting? Was it at school? Did you get in trouble?"

"I bet it was over some girl," Aunt Sis says, shaking her head at my stupidity and maybe at the stupidity of males in general.

I hold the warm washrag on the back of my head. "It wasn't at school, and it wasn't over a girl. It was at work. With my boss."

"You fought your boss?" Mama Sally says. It's the only time in my life I've seen her look shocked. "Your *white* boss?"

I nod. "I did. But he started it." I tell them about Mr. Stevens tearing the pages out of the Nat Turner book and flushing them down the toilet.

"Junebug,"—Mama Sally's voice sounds sorrowful—"it wasn't right what that white man did, but you can't come in swinging every time a white man hurts your pride some way. If you do, you're never gonna stop fighting."

"Not till you run into the wrong white man and he kills you," Aunt Sis adds. She's never been one to mince words.

"That's right," Mama Sally says. "Besides, the Bible says to turn the other cheek."

"Well, he would've hit that cheek too," I say.

"Did you get fired?" Mama Sally asks.

"No, I didn't. I wanted to run off after it happened, but then I thought, how would I pay the rent? How would I eat? It also seemed kind of mean to leave Maurice and Sharon to finish the shift short one person, so I just kept on working. I didn't see Mr. Stevens for the rest of the shift. I reckon he went off to hide and lick his wounds like a dog."

"Well, if you were gonna fight him, I'm glad you at least got your licks in," Aunt Sis says, and Mama Sally shoots her a disapproving look.

Sitting there with Mama Sally and Aunt Sis, I'm surprised to feel tears spring to my eyes. They're both such sources of strength, and strength is what I need right now. "You know," I say, "I couldn't keep on living with Daddy and Miss May because I felt so full of anger all the time; it was like it was eating me up."

"I know, baby," Mama Sally says, taking my hand and holding it.

"Leaving was the right decision," I say. "I think it might be this time too."

"Sometimes, it's all you can do," Mama Sally says.

I nod. "I've started saving all the money I can because I feel like after graduation, I might need to leave. For real."

"Leave Vicksburg?" Aunt Sis asks.

I swallow hard. "Leave Mississippi. Leave the whole South." *Leave everybody I've ever known and loved,* I think, but I can't say this part out loud because if I do, I'll cry too hard to talk. "It seems like if you stay here, especially if you're a man, Jim Crow's gonna get you one way or the other.

Starve you to death because you can't get a decent job. Get you beaten to death or shot or hung. Or just eat you up from the inside so you have to drink to numb the pain like Daddy does. The longer I stay here, the madder I get, and the madder I get, the more likely I am to get myself in a situation there's no walking away from. I feel like if I stay here, I'll die."

Now Mama Sally's crying too. "I understand. You're feisty, always have been. Why should you stay somewhere that feistiness is gonna be beat out of you?" She takes a tissue that Aunt Sis offers her and dabs at her eyes. "You know, your daddy's sisters is out in Seattle. One of them might give you a room if you asked them. I've never been one to think that moving away solves all your problems because some of your problems are gonna come with you. But I know Old Jim Crow won't come with you if you move to Seattle. He's gonna stay right here."

I try to imagine moving all the way across the country. "Seattle, huh? I don't even know what that'd be like."

"They say it's real different from here. Nice," Aunt Sis says. "Mama Sally and me, we're talking about moving there one day too."

"Is that a fact?" I say. I can't picture Mama Sally and Aunt Sis living anywhere but this house. But the thought of them being in Seattle, too, makes me feel braver.

"We've been talking about it," Mama Sally says. "Sis, why don't you go get the address book? Junebug needs to write his Aunt Fran a letter."

"So in Seattle?" I say. "They got colleges out there? Because I've been thinking I might want to go to college."

Mama Sally smiles. "Yes, they've got 'em. My Junebug, a college man. Now, wouldn't that be something?" We sit in silence for a moment, then she says, "You know, we called you Junebug because you was born in the summer when the June bugs come out. When I was a little girl, we used to play with June bugs like toys. We'd catch them and tie a piece of string around one of their legs and hang onto the other end of the string and fly them around like little kites, listening to them buzz. We were just kids, you know, so we never thought about how the June bugs felt or if we was hurting them. One day, my mama saw me with a June bug on a string and said, 'You need to cut that thing loose.' I asked her why, and she said, 'Because it's one of God's creatures. You don't have the right to tie it up and tell it where it can and can't go. It needs to fly free.'" Mama Sally squeezes my hand. "That's what you need, too, Junebug. You need to fly free."

18
MOVING FORWARD

"That hat doesn't want to stay on, does it?" Mama Sally is adjusting my graduation cap one last time before I get in line with the other graduates.

"No, it keeps sliding around," I say. "I don't know why they made a hat this stupid for something that's supposed to prove you're smart."

Daddy, who's standing beside Mama Sally, laughs. "Well, you worked awful hard for the right to wear that stupid hat, so try to keep it on your head."

I find my place in the line. I feel nervous—what if I trip over this gown and fall when I go up to get my diploma?—but I feel proud too. Not just proud of myself but proud of the other young men and women in line with me. It hasn't been easy for any of us, but here we are.

The music teacher starts playing "Pomp and Circumstance" on the piano, and we go into the auditorium and march down the aisle. I only have to adjust my hat once.

It's hard for me to concentrate on what's being said on the stage because I'm so full of disbelief about where I am right now and where I'm going in the near future. Graduating, then moving to Seattle to live with Aunt Francis and Uncle Cecil, then starting classes at Seattle Community College, where I've already been accepted. I'm going places, literally, and running out of Jim Crow's reach. Aunt Sis says there's prejudice everywhere, and I'm sure she's right. But at least I can live somewhere where it's not the law of the land.

We stand up for the hymn "Lift Every Voice and Sing," which often gets called The Negro National Anthem. I've sung it a lot in school and at church, too, but there's something different about it today because I really pay attention to the words.

Sing a song full of the faith that the dark past has taught us
Sing a song full of the hope that the present has brought us
Facing the rising sun of our new day begun
Let us march on till victory is won.

As we sing, I feel like I'm hearing not just the voices of the friends and family surrounding me but also all the voices of my people—past, present, and future, all the way back to Africa and all the way forward to who knows where. I feel the presence of those who came before me and those who will come after me.

But the strongest presence I feel is Mama. Her love covers me like a suit of armor to protect me from the arrows of injustice. I will wear it always.

VICKSBURG, MISSISSIPPI

———

1969

19

A WARNING

One evening after work, James comes to visit me at the Y in downtown Vicksburg. I am lounging and reading a book in the small room I rent. James knocks on the door three times, and we exchange pleasantries.

"What's up JW?" I call him JW to uncork James the man, versus James Washington, the new manager of KFC on Clay street.

JW delivers the news that Mr. Stevens is complaining to Detective Johnson of the Vicksburg Police about my recent behavior. He warns me to be careful and watch my back.

"You cannot put your head in the sand on this one," he says sternly.

I respond, "I am finishing school and working on my goals, JW."

James steps closer and lowers his voice. "You got to listen; I overheard something you need to pay attention to. Mr. Stevens was talking to D. J. They were talking about you forgetting your place, disrespecting, and being uppity—starting fights with white men."

JW's words make me agitated, like an old washing machine in a basement.

I agree with James by nodding and saying, "Thanks James for the heads up. I'll be careful."

Mr. Stevens and Detective Johnson have a friendship that goes way back, and the two of them talking about me forgetting my place is bad news.

"See you tomorrow," I say.

Hoping to benefit from a good night's sleep, I go to bed, but nightmares follow me. Restless images flash through my dreams: Emmett Till's smiling face from under the brim of a jaunty hat faded into a bloody, unrecognizable face lying in a coffin. It doesn't stop there. Singular snapshots, one of a body swinging from a leafless tree, another of one hanging from a country bridge silhouetted against the light of dawn, surge through my mind like frames on a newsreel. In the dream, I try to escape the images but find myself paralyzed, flattened against a brick wall under a "No Colored Allowed" sign. A mob of angry men moves closer until I feel hard ridges against my ribs. I have nowhere to go.

Wet with sweat, unable to forget the pictures or shake off the fear, I lie in the darkness wishing I could escape into sleep but afraid of what I might see.

Stop it, I tell myself. *I'm in my room at the Y, and I'm letting my imagination run wild. Calm down.*

Trying to think of a way to change my focus, I remember the book *Coming of Age in Mississippi,* by Anne Moody. She wrote about her experiences growing up poor, female, and Black in rural Mississippi. She said her poor childhood made her ". . . angry enough to get involved to change her circumstances, rather than live as a victim of her circumstances." Her words inspire me to turn the nightmares into dreams.

I know from the newspapers at the colored library that my own problems are part of a much bigger struggle that is sweeping Mississippi and the rest of America.

I think about the Civil Rights Movement through a different lens, wondering about the conversations I overhear at the segregated school, the segregated Y where I now live, and the articles I read at the colored library. Where are the NAACP, CORE, AND SNCC in Vicksburg?

Ever since the fight at the Kentucky Fried Chicken, restless sleep and worry haunt me. I can't forget the anger that possessed my body when Mr. Stevens ripped out the pages from *Nat Turner,* or the fear in Mama Sally's voice when she heard what I'd done.

Tonight, after the warning and nightmares, I lie in this bed and shake. Too tired and on edge to sleep, I pull out my journal. There is no place to go, and no one to talk to. Maybe getting some of the thinking out of my head and onto a page will help me sleep. I began.

>   Mr. Stevens is up to no good. We all know that he's a snake in the grass. He's facing his last days as the kitchen manager. Last week at the staff meeting, the owner made it clear that he wasn't happy with sales and production. James is taking over Mr. Stevens' job. James deserves it because he worked hard and smart and was always present when the heat turned up in the kitchen. After all, Mr. Stevens was gone most of the time and left all the work for James, Melvin, and me. James promotes harmony, and Mr. Stevens promotes disharmony and rancor in the kitchen. The KFC is a vital business in the community. It supports sports teams on both sides of town, and the teams buy a lot of chicken. James knows how to cater to the Sunday church crowd, regardless of background. James makes plenty of green for the owner. I'll never forget the day that the owner told me in the hallway that Melvin, James, and I helped him make his first million dollars.
>
>   How can I turn my back on my family and fulfill my promise to Mama? Does that make me a coward? But what are the chances I won't survive to help anyone if I stay? I know the history of Mississippi and how people like me get found months later in the Tallahatchie River face down. I know a warning is a warning, especially in Mississippi. In Richard Wright's novel Native Son, Bigger Thomas couldn't let go of the demons. The anger and hate took him over and followed him from Mississippi to Chicago in 1948, and here it is, over twenty years later, and that anger and hate are grinding up my guts just like it did with him. It is too exhausting carrying this weight, but what can I do? Maybe moving on is the answer. Once I get an education

and grow up some more, I can be a part of the movement and make a difference for my sisters and their children, but for now, I just need to survive and get an education . . . not a separate left-over education, but the real deal.

I nudge myself, trying to stay awake to write more, and realize that is silly. The point of writing is to ease into sleep. I might as well stop and close my eyes. After closing the journal, I sleep deeply.

20

FRIDAY NIGHT FOOTBALL

It's the weekend before Thanksgiving and beautiful. The little one-street downtown is buzzing with talk of the big game. Football is a special religion in Mississippi. Friday night, Saturday, and Sunday all day.

James, Melvin, and I have a whopping time cooking the last pots of yard bird for the evening. We finish our shift at the KFC around 7:00 p.m. Friday night is guys' night out, and we have plans to visit Kitchen in the Garden, the local soul food place. We're looking forward to getting some cold drinks and eating some neighborhood food.

The Kitchen is only three blocks away if we take the shortcut through St Mary's campus, but there is a problem. The game is at St. Mary's, and we aren't welcome on the campus. We should walk six blocks out of our way if we want to stay out of trouble. So we're heading out the long way when Melvin suddenly starts for the shortcut. I hesitate, feeling the hair prickle on the back of my neck. *Isn't this the big game night? Against Vicksburg High? Might be some folks looking for trouble.*

Melvin must have read my mind. "They'll all be heading home by now. Don't be getting all scaredy cats on us now, Junebug," he said.

"Hey man, you're not out in the woods where they pump daylight anymore," said JW.

Those two always enjoyed teasing me about being from the country.

The three of us set us a path across the campus. It doesn't take long to know everybody hasn't gone home. Angry voices, heavy with liquor, fill the air, complaining. Apparently, they had lost to a team with one Black player, the quarterback.

Melvin, James, and I already knew there might be trouble. Then we hear a belligerent voice rise above the others. "The white girls were all over that—" There is that not-so-nice word again.

A clear warning. I knew any form of integration of the races is unnerving to the middle-age folk who live in a town where many still proudly fly the Confederate flag.

A beer bottle shatters in the path near us.

We step up our pace, keeping a downward gaze, and do our best to maneuver through the maze of campus pathways without attracting attention. As we hurry, I think of Ralph Ellison's *Invisible Man* and wish we could pass unseen. And I try to unhear the nasty language going on all around us.

Scattered groups of disgruntled fans loiter in the walkways, making it hard to walk three abreast, so me and Melvin and James walk single-file, just trying to keep our heads down and hustle without running.

In the darkness, I don't see the man bundled up in a dark coat and bump into him. He takes a step back to steady himself. A gooey wad of tobacco hits my forehead and its slime slides down my face, off my chin, and onto my white KFC shirt. The wet juice seeps through my shirt to my skin.

The man expels a stream of abusive language. My mind races.

Not today. I'd rather fight than hide. I'm tired of kissing up to rude people, and I will not apologize.

"Dirty [*there's that word again*], that's what you get for forgetting your place. You got no right here on this campus. Get your uppity selves out of here! Y'all wanna fight? Come on, show me whatcha got," he hisses.

I'd been in danger before. A fellow pulled a gun on me once, and I can still hear the gang's uncontrolled laughter after I collapsed and cried for Mama. The memory crashes into the present moment, and my self-control evaporates. I feel my body flood with heat, and I want to smash my fist through the man's nose. I just don't care about anything else.

James and Melvin press against me. Calm, reasonable voices tell me to stop and think.

"Leave it alone, Junebug."

"Come on along now."

"Just walk away."

"Leave it, Junebug."

With clenched fists and feet planted ready to lunge, everything inside me wants to push them away. But I let them lead me away. Their soft words, all worried-sounding and logical, gradually soothe me, just like Mama Sally's the night when she warned me after my fight with Mr. Stevens. I'm suddenly back there, feeling the warm cloth she pressed against my cheek and smelling the cornbread fresh from the oven.

It's hard to be composed when you have been spit on, but I know then that I have to allow myself to be led away. I've learned how to swallow my pride in Mississippi. Aunt Sis would have something to say about that.

Later, back at the Y, still shaken, I don't even bother to lie down before reaching for my journal. I might not describe the whole evening, but I could at least try to find words to help me understand what was going on in my mind and body.

> Tonight could have gone a different way. Leaving, getting an education, helping my family, all my hopes and dreams would have meant nothing. I might have ended up in jail or swinging from the bridge, all because I took a shortcut. I got spit on and insulted and somehow found the strength to walk away. One more warning. I'm sick and tired of being sick and tired of seeing no way for my dreams: tired of watching CBS with rabbit ears; tired working for Colonel Sanders with his white suit; tired of having to worry about offending someone every time I step outside.

I miss Mama, her hugs, her face, her love and feel alone and afraid that one of those thugs will come looking for me. I know I have opportunities and choices out west, but here in Mississippi . . . Here, I don't have the contacts or connections to get into Jackson State, Alcorn, or MVSC. I have Utica Community College for a back-up plan. It's a trade school where I can learn a trade and get a low-paying job but not an education that will advance my mind. Why am I putting it off? Maybe enough is enough. It's time to buy my bus ticket and move on.

I sleep.

The next morning, still feeling determined, shaken, and a little worried about giving up a steady paycheck, I get busy. I pull $223.78 from under my mattress, enough to buy a ticket with a little left over. I walk out of the colored YMCA and head for the bus station where I buy a bus ticket. *Even though I won't be using it until June, at least I'll have it. From now on I'll be looking west and saving my money.*

The family up north offers an opportunity. I could make something of myself or stay in Mississippi and wind up a high school graduate, picking cotton the rest of my live. Here, the community college offers me a chance to learn a skill that will get me a job. I'll be using my body and my hands but not my mind. In Seattle, I can get a college degree and read about history and politics. I want to use my brain. I want to be part of the change that is sweeping the country. From now on, I'll watch my back until I get enough money saved to climb up the stairs of the Greyhound bus and start a new future in Seattle.

21

THE JOURNEY BEGINS

JUNE 1, 1969

I join the passengers funneling through the gate toward the Greyhound bus. In ten minutes, we'd all leave the Vicksburg station.

I clutched Mama Sally's store-bought suitcase in one hand and my ticket in the other, allowing my feet to take me to the bus proudly as I hum, "These Boots Are Made for Walkin'" by Nancy Sinatra.

I am living in the moment, moving forward and leaving home behind. I hope to never have to deal with Mississippi ruffians again.

Sight unseen, I lean on a hope and a prayer about Seattle, buoyed by this feeling I have that all will be well. I'll get a new job and new friends. Some folks have to visit a place first and move later. I guess that's not in my DNA. I feel ready to step into the unknown.

As I move through the line, I remember Robert Frost's line, "... *a road less traveled ... and I took the one less traveled by, and that has made all the difference.*"

"All aboard!"

Relief and a sense of freedom flow through my body. I continue following the crowd, step onto the bus, and look for a seat. *I can take any seat that I want*, I realize. A seat in the middle section, a seat by the window, is open. I sit.

The diesel engine shakes the bus, but we don't move. Workers are still loading the storage compartment. I notice a woman rushing on board, and that's when I realize the aisle seat beside me is the last available seat.

Will she expect me to move to the aisle seat? To stand? I had enjoyed the freedom of picking my own seat, and now there is a wave of dread as I realize the bus driver might make me move. Last year, on a trip to Detroit, the driver forced me to give up my seat on a Jim Crow bus. That feeling is still hard to push down.

The white lady smiles and slips into the seat beside me. I smile back and glance down at my book as I clutch my journal.

I desperately want to scribble a few notes and remain incognito.

Before I get started, the lady introduces herself and offers her hand. "Hi, I'm Bonnie Smith."

I hesitate, then smile. *I guess I'm making friends already.*

And we shook hands, a white woman and a Black man. "I'm Wilson Reed Jr., but everyone calls me Junebug."

She smiles. "Junebug! You have a bright smile. Is that why they call you that?"

"I don't know, ma'am. People here just come up with names that stick."

"So, Junebug, what brings you here on this bus today? Are you heading off to school, a new job, or visiting relatives?"

I'm surprised to be asked so many pointed questions all at once. Old habits are causing me to feel a bit suspicious, but maybe this is how some white folks talk. Her smile and open manner help me relax. I explain, in as polite of words as I can muster, that I'm doing a little of all three, heading for Seattle, Washington. I try to turn the conversation to her. In doing so, I let down my guard and engage with her.

I figure meeting people will help to take the edge off the 2,600-mile trip.

"Miss Bonnie, I'm curious to know what brings you here today."

"Junebug,"—she still sounds nice—"I came out here, all the way from Los Angeles, to visit my son. He's stationed near Biloxi on the Gulf Coast." She adds, "I'm a history teacher and wanted to visit the Vicksburg battle site. In Dallas, I'm catching a plane back to California."

She continues, "I earned my history degree from UCLA and thought I knew all about the siege of Vicksburg, but since I walked through the park, I faced the gravity of the battle and lost lives on both sides. I realized I know nothing about Mulligan's Bend. Have you ever been to the battlefield?"

I tell her I have limited information about the site.

I know it's a tourist attraction, along with the casinos. Strangers and visitors coming and going daily downtown. There was that time Melvin had seen a bunch of white guys running around with Confederate-gray outfits on, playing war games. Me and Melvin had laughed until we cried. Other than that, I hadn't given the place much thought, except as a torturous place to run when we'd tried out for track.

Coach Adams provided the team with maximum exposure. Twenty students tried out for the track team in Spring 1968. We all got a tour of the battlefield by running over the hills and rocky terrain. It was a highly competitive tryout, and the memory of baking in the Mississippi sun while running and jumping my heart out collides with my memory of hoping to make the team.

I tell Miss Bonnie how I wanted to excel like Aunt Emma did at the 1948 Olympics, where she won a bronze medal in Rome. I had a fantasy of being a long jumper or running the mile in record time.

Daddy's sister, Aunt Emma, was my role model and the first person who taught me how to fish at the pond behind the family shack. She is from little Redwood, Mississippi, too, a place so small it doesn't even have a post office.

I tell Miss Bonnie that my high school, Temple, was named after a Black woman and had produced its share of sports stars and academics in Mississippi.

For some unknown reason, I had dreamed of becoming a star and famous on TV, like Flip Wilson. I even told Miss Bonnie that I had never wanted to live life as a poor guy who worked on a farm and picked cotton to make money for the rest of his life.

In telling my story, I focus on the courage it took to try out and meet the great Coach Adams. I knew knowledge is power and wanted some of the knowledge the coach shared with strangers and players in town.

Coach Adams cares about the whole student athlete and wants young people to go out and make a difference in the world after graduation. He is a national speaker for VISTA too. I've always found the coach inspirational.

I said, "Miss Bonnie, I don't know if you remember seeing the hills and trails that are covered with old roots and stones, but it is a hard trail for track. Coach Adams figured making us run up and down those bumpy hills would help him figure out who he wanted on his team. A couple of guys thought they'd pull one over on Coach and pretended to run the course, but hid at the bottom. He caught them and made them run it again, following them in his Opal. When it was all over, Coach gave us all a lecture, telling us, 'Losers never win, and winners never cheat!'"

Bonnie nods and smiles with her full attention to the whole telling.

We share a good laugh, then Bonnie says, "Junebug, that is very good advice, thank you. You are a wonderful storyteller and a wise young man."

We continue to talk, and I learn about Bonnie's family, where they live in Los Angeles, and how she worries about her son going off to Vietnam to fight. She is proud and worried, a mother's worry that is intensified by the pictures on the nightly news.

I talk about growing up on a cotton farm and moving to the city but leave out the sad parts.

We talk all the way from Vicksburg to Shreveport, where the bus pulls into the station for a quick break.

Once back on board, we chat a little more before we both turn to our books and, within a few minutes, nod off to sleep. Imagine that, sleeping next to each other on a bus.

We arrive at the station in Dallas at dinnertime. Bonnie wishes me good luck, and I think she really means it.

"Goodbye," I say. "I'll send up prayers for your son." Once again, she offers her hand.

I know Texas is a big state, and it will be a long time before we cross into Oklahoma. It's time to fulfill my promise to Aunt Fran and use some of my quarters to let her know how far I have come.

The big station has bathrooms, a cafeteria, and a special section of pay phones. After visiting the men's room, I spy an open phone and insert a fist-full of quarters for a call to Seattle.

Aunt Fran's voice is full of energy and encouragement. "Junebug! It's good to hear from you. Where are you?"

I tell her about the bus station and about meeting a nice lady. She asks me about what I am eating and tells me to pick up some oranges to eat on the bus to help hold me over. I promise her I'll be careful and get some snacks.

They are planning a big Reed family reunion for when I arrive, and Aunt Fran tells me they'll have surprises, so I better stay healthy and keep on the right path. "I love you, Junebug."

It seems like it's time to say goodbye before we've barely said hello, and I reluctantly hang up the phone, feeling a strange mix of hope, regret, happiness, and loneliness. The feelings buzz in my stomach as I stand by a payphone in the biggest bus station I ever could have imagined, smack in the middle of Dallas, Texas.

I walk toward a newsstand that's selling oranges and sodas and peel a dollar from my wallet, already understanding it is best to take Aunt Fran's advice.

Back on the bus, I find my same seat and pull out my journal. It will be another thirty-five minutes before the engine starts and we head out on the new interstate. The bus moves out and aims for the bridge just as the morning light sheds a golden glow on the river. We ride on it until we hit Fort Worth.

Feelings stirring, I'm grateful to have a way to settle down. Miss Watson's words come back as if she is sitting there beside me. "It is important to write your thoughts down in a journal or keep notes in a special place. You're a ship without a rudder without your memories. Memories—keep them alive and tell their stories. Keep them always treasured in your heart and soul."

I made a new friend, talked to Aunt Fran, and am headed north. I'm getting a solid dose of kindness, and it's sweeping out the ugly memories that pushed me away from home. My new friend is a lady from Los Angeles and knows more about the Vicksburg siege than I ever thought there was to know. I lived my whole life here and only thought of the place as a brutal place to run from. Her kindness reminded me of Mama.

22

WARNED AGAIN

I wake up feeling the bus rattle to a stop. The bus driver calls out, "Oklahoma City!"

I've heard about Oklahoma City from one of my favorite authors, Ralph Ellison, who wrote *The Invisible Man* and grew up in the city.

"Boy, you might need to get yourself a cowboy hat riding the bus through Texas and Oklahoma." A tall Texan slips into the aisle seat beside me. "I'm Withers. Guess I'll be your next-door neighbor till I get to my stop."

The man's height is the first thing I notice, so I'm thinking he is probably happy to have a seat where he can stretch a leg out into the aisle. I mind my own business when I see the Confederate flag patch on the man's jacket pocket. I inch closer to the window, where I try to look real interested in my book.

My plan doesn't work. Withers keeps on with his yacking and smells like chewing tobacco. Even has the brown teeth to go with it.

"You'll need to buy yourself a cowboy hat, boy, at the next stop," Withers repeats himself.

I wonder for about five seconds. *What would I look like in a Stetson hat?* But I still don't engage and just listen, keeping a safe distance in my seat. *Just when I think I can leave some of those memories behind, I meet someone determined to put me in my place.* I continue musing, *What did I do to bring this dude into my life?*

Withers uses rude names when he complains about the Mexicans and laments the good ole days, "... where everyone knew his or her place ..." He goes on and on about problems with women's rights, farmworker unions, and civil rights.

Is this guy trying to bait me into a fight? I wonder. *Even if I had a Dallas cowboy outfit on, Withers would bug me for fun.*

Everyone is quiet on the bus, but Withers still goes on talking loud and boastful.

By the time we reach the panhandle, I am sick and tired of Withers's voice and speak up for the first time. "I want to ride in peace and will get a different seat at the next stop on the long ride through Oklahoma."

With the words, I look directly into Withers's eyes, feeling determined. "My dad was a Marine and fought for this country. He was a good soldier and still proudly wears his uniform at parades and funerals."

Withers peers at me and sinks back into his seat, holding his transistor radio and sucking on a wad of tobacco through his teeth.

I'm free to speak my mind and stand up for myself, I remind myself as worry floods my blood.

When nothing else happens, I relax and enjoy the trip without getting into a row with the man called Withers.

At Wichita Falls, Withers pulls down his big, green Army surplus bag and strides off the bus. Thankfully, he isn't going on to the Northwest. I pull out my journal and think what a relief it is to write my thoughts and move past the mess of feelings I've been having so I can sleep.

Before closing my eyes, I reflect on this uncomfortable meeting.

I can't believe I just told a white man to mind his own business and that I feel good about it. I guess I should count myself lucky that I only had to spend a whole day sitting next to a tobacco-chewing jerk who wore the Confederate flag and was cruising for a bruising. Jim Crow might give some people the idea that they can talk anyway they want, but this time, he didn't keep me from speaking my mind.

I wish JW and Melvin could have seen me telling Withers to back off. They were so surprised when I said I was working my last shift until I told them I was afraid for my life. Then I saw they understood. Neither of them graduated from high school, and they're both stuck at the bottom of the service industry with no prospects, having to kowtow to Mr. Stevens. Maybe the changes that are coming will help them find hope as managers.

Withers isn't that different from that drunk at St. Mary's. Luckily, I let JW and Melvin lead me away. This time, I stayed calm and used my words to say what I needed. Who knows how it would have ended if I hadn't lost my temper and started beating on Mr. Stevens or gotten into a fight with Daddy? Something in me just snapped. I'm learning to use my brains now, trying to follow the teachings of Dr. King. Still and all, I can't help wondering about that question from my logic class: "When will individuals with closed minds wake up and smell the coffee?"

23

THE HIPPIE

After another day, the bus arrives in Denver. Since Lubbock, I've mostly had the two seats to myself, giving me extra room to slip in and out of sleep during the monotonous drive through the desert.

A big map of the interstate bus routes of the United States takes up most of a wall at the station. I can see how far I've come from Redwood to Denver, and how far I still have to go. From here, we'll be heading over the Rockies, west to Utah, then north to Idaho, and finally, west to Seattle. I feel disheveled and tired, but seeing how far I've come gives me a burst of energy. The rest of the trip is due north. I meander to the men's room to wash my face, brush my teeth, and straighten myself up before using my quarters to call Aunt Fran.

At the sound of Aunt Fran's voice, I smile and push back tears. It's as bright and encouraging as ever. "Where are you?" she wants to know.

"Denver."

She yells at Uncle Cecil. "Cecil, Junebug's almost home! We got to start planning his welcome party!"

I tell my aunt about traveling through Texas, the way forward, and how I've been meeting interesting folks. Words fall out in a stream of excitement. I guess they've been bottled up since I stepped foot on the bus in Vicksburg.

I go on until the operator interrupts me and tells me to insert five more quarters.

"Junebug, that's enough talk for now. We'll have plenty of time to catch up on Saturday. You just stay safe. Drink lots of water. Can't wait till I get to see you and wrap you up in a big bear hug.

"Yes, ma'am." That's all I can say because the phone clicks off, and the line goes dead.

Those old grasshoppers are at it again, making me feel jittery and out of sorts. But new feelings of hope and love enter the mix—good and unfamiliar at the same time. I go back to my seat by the window and try to settle down, realizing that what I've been working for is really happening. I, Wilson Reed Jr., am heading to a new family in a free land.

The new passengers start climbing up the steps. Curious about who might be my next seatmate, I watch as they enter the bus. There is one unusually tall woman with wide shoulders and a head of long, curly red hair. I soon realize the person is a young *man*. I had seen hippies on TV but never in person. I decide right there that I want to rid myself of stereotypes. What a job undoing tapes from early childhood.

The bus driver's voice blares over the microphone. "Next stop, Boise, Idaho, then Yakima, Washington. Last stop, Seattle—in thirty-two hours and twenty-eight minutes."

The new passengers begin finding their seats. Then the engines start, and I feel a bit of surprise when the hippie stops at my seat, nods, and asks, "Mind if I sit here?"

"Go right ahead."

"Cool, I'm Jerry."

"Nice to meet you. I'm Wilson, but I go by Junebug."

The hippie—I mean, the man—hoists his backpack onto the rack and swings into the seat.

Jerry starts talking to me right off, like we've known each other since high school. I learn Jerry is on a long trip from Colorado to Portland, changing buses in Pendleton. I learn a lot about war and protest from listening to Jerry, about how he's marched for the peace movement. Even though he's been in jail, he isn't giving up. Jerry says, "I'll keep protesting against the draft until the war ends. I'm on my way to a demonstration in Portland."

Jerry also tells me about his childhood. Raised as a Quaker, he's spent his whole life focusing on peace and non-violence. His father worked as a medic during World War II, a conscientious objector, because Quakers won't fight in a war. Jerry explains to me that if he gets drafted, he will do the same thing, but in the meantime, he'll be fighting against the draft because he believes it's wrong to force people to kill each other. That people should stand up against violence.

Much of Jerry's talk sounds like the words of Dr. Martin Luther King. Jerry even spoke of his admiration for Dr. King. And I like that.

So I share part of my story, that I am a working-class guy, moving to Seattle for opportunities to work, go to school, and live with family folks.

"Congratulations on taking the big step to escape Southern oppression."

That is a new one for me. I've always just thought of it as Jim Crow,, the boogie man that chases you on the playground and sets you up for trouble with "gotcha rules." I've never thought about being oppressed..

Spurred on by his affirmation, I tell Jerry about my old hunting buddy, Robert Scott, who volunteered in the Army and came back home in a wooden box six months later. I am still close with the Scott family, and from time to time, I speak with his daddy, Pat Scott, who never has come to grips with the death of his son. Strong feelings rile up inside me. I turn my face away and look out the window, trying to make sense of it all. I consider writing in my journal about Robert, the war, and even about Daddy. How did fighting in the war affect my daddy?

But it's now getting dark, and I am tired.

The bus keeps pushing north. Though now we're also heading west. An exit sign approaches through the window, and I read it as it flashes by: "Salt Lake City, 95 miles."

My eyes slip closed, and I move toward sleep in peace. Before drifting completely off, I think about how Jerry is totally different from what I imagined when I type casted him in the line of new passengers miles earlier.

As we are crossing the Rockies, me and Jerry start up our conversation again. We share stories about our families and get around to talking about our mutual love of reading. Jerry shows me the book *War and Peace* by Leo Tolstoy.

"This old book tells it all," he says. I had never read a book that big.

"I'll look for that one in the library once I get to Seattle," I said.

A few hours later, the bus carrying all us tired folk arrive in Pendleton, Oregon, Jerry's transfer point. We part as friends.

Jerry smiles when he says, "Good luck in finding a living-wage job in Seattle."

I return his grin and reply, "Best of luck on the march and recruitment of peaceniks."

I just said goodbye to Jerry. It's sad that I may never see him again, but now when I listen to the news about the war, I'll remember Jerry. I never heard so much about peace and Gandhi from anyone besides Martin Luther King, and that was on an old, crackling black-and-white TV with a bad picture and rabbit ears. I came close to dismissing Jerry, but now I realize how much more I know and understand because of our conversation. All that talk about how young white people with long hair are peaceniks, communists, dirty drug addicts, and lazy had me almost ready to ignore him. I almost believed the talk before I knew the man. It just goes to show you can't believe everything you hear.

When I started out on this bus ride, all I could think about was how long it would take to get to where I was going, how

I'd pass the time, and how hungry I'd get. Now, I've seen a lot of different parts of the USA and met a lot of different people. I'm still looking forward to getting settled with my Seattle family, starting school, and finding a job, but I'm also getting to enjoy seeing the country and the people. As I understand the different ways that people look at things, I get questions and start learning all kinds of things. I'm understanding that if I think I know someone based on how they look, before I've even talked to them, I'm usually wrong.

The bus travels with the rising sun north from Pendleton. We speed across the Columbia River, past farmland dotted with green irrigation circles, through small farm towns, and climb up the Cascade Mountains into the clouds. As soon as the bus passes the summit, I notice the air is cool and heavy with moisture. A wall of fir trees flanks the highway, and the bus speeds past clusters of neon signs advertising restaurants and motels. Seattle emerges, framed in the window, surrounded by white mountain peaks and sparkling blue water. Soon, I will meet up with Aunt Fran for the first time in many years.

SEATTLE, WASHINGTON

———

1969

24

KINFOLK PARTY

The bus station is downtown, and when I walk off the bus, I am ecstatic to see Aunt Fran and Uncle Cecil waiting for me in the lobby.

"Welcome, Junebug Wilson!" they call. Aunt Fran rushes up and throws her arms around me in a bear hug, just like she promised. Uncle Cecil waits beside her, smiling. I'm feeling totally embarrassed and nervous, but the welcome is so good that feelings of relief take over. It actually feels like I've come home.

Aunt Fran and Uncle Cecil usher me out of the bus station and down the street to their Oldsmobile. The '66 Oldsmobile is parked on a hill, wedged between two other cars. "Now, all we have to do is survive Uncle Cecil's driving through the streets of Seattle," jokes Aunt Fran.

At least I think she is kidding, but I soon find out that riding with Uncle Cecil is as much an act of faith as taking a bus ride all the way from Mississippi!

Uncle Cecil grips the steering wheel with both hands and forcefully turns it to the right. He lays his foot on the gas, and we surge into traffic, causing a taxi to honk and jerk to a stop behind us. We speed forward, nearly slamming into the delivery truck waiting for the light.

Aunt Fran warns her husband, "Cecil, lighten up that foot and lay off the accelerator."

105

But it doesn't work. I pull in a breath and hold it until it explodes out of my chest when he makes a sudden stop at Second and Boren.

Aunt Fran ignores her husband's driving and launches into the role of travel guide and historian. She bellows over the noise of the busy port city, "There's the Space Needle and the Seattle Science Center with the white arches. We'll be crossing a bridge pretty soon where you'll be able to see the University of Washington. Aunt Mary has some information to get you into that school this September. Down that way is Boeing, where you're gonna get a job this summer. We're heading for the CD, that's what we call the Central District, the part of the city where we live. It's also the home of Quincy Jones, Jimi Hendrix, and Reverend Adams of FAME Church. This city is changing, and you got yourself here at just the right time."

When they arrive at Aunt Fran's, my body is shaking from the drive, and I don't notice all the cars parked in their driveway.

I enter a house filled with family and the smell of good cooking. There is a big pitcher of cherry Kool-Aid, along with bowls of macaroni and cheese, greens, chili, molded salads with marshmallows, potato salad, and a big sheet cake decorated with the words, "Welcome Home Junebug Wilson!"

Gladys Knight's *I Heard it Through the Grapevine* is playing on the radio. Everybody's standing in a reception line, smiling and waiting to greet me. I feel like a star.

Moving down the line, I grip hands, hug, and smile until my cheeks hurt. Then, at the end, is the biggest surprise of all. There is Mama Sally, wearing a beautiful lavender dress! She'd flown up from Mississippi the same day I left on the bus! They were all planning a big Reed family reunion for the Fourth of July, two days after my eighteenth birthday.

The food is delicious, and I ate until my belly is full. My aunts keep bringing extra servings, but I'm not sure how much more I can fit in my stomach. Though, they remark about how I make the women proud with how much I can eat.

Stories and laughter fill the dining room. I especially enjoy the stories about Daddy before he went off to war. The stories sound like they are about someone I've never met, and it gets me wondering, *Does going to war change a person that much?*

A chiming ensues. Aunt Fran is hitting her spoon against her Kool-Aid glass. My other aunties get busy hushing the room full of family until pretty soon, there is a grand silence.

"I rarely make speeches, but today, the Lord has brought us a very special gift. He reached all the way back down to the old Mississippi and delivered Junebug Wilson."

Her voice grows stronger and louder, and the rest of the room responds like they do for the preacher on Sunday mornings, offering responses like, "Yes, ma'am!" and "Uh, huh!"

She continues, "Junebug, y'all listen up! We're all here so you know we love you and are looking forward to seeing you prosper."

Her words arrest me like nothing I've ever heard, or at least not heard since my Mama died back in 1964.

"Boy, I like you a lot, and I am going to treat you like the son I never had."

There is a hush until Uncle Cecil makes everyone laugh when he says, "I thought we were gettin' cake!"

June 5, 1969

I'm here at Aunt Fran's and Uncle Cecil's. Tonight, I'll be sleeping in my own room. I'm going to bed soon with a full stomach and clean sheets. Seattle is a far cry from Vicksburg. That is easy to see, but it will take a few weeks before I understand everything she was explaining to me. One thing I know for sure, Aunt Fran is going to be lighting a fire under me to get moving.

Today was like a big, old-fashioned homecoming. Love wrapped me up in a big quilt of love I haven't felt since Mama died. After everyone left, the three of us sat down at the kitchen table for a glass of milk. Aunt Fran delivered a speech—one that I keep reciting in my brain over and over again.

She said, "Boy, what's mine is yours. You are the son I always wanted. Come and go in and out of the house freely, eat food in the fridge, and shoot pool until eleven o'clock at night. You can use the upstairs or downstairs bathroom."

I'd never heard the words, "What is mine is yours," and didn't understand what she meant. Then there was the word 'boy.' That bothered me for about five minutes until I understood she was telling me she loves me and wants to help me. She meant it in a kind way, not the 'you ain't nothing' way that I heard when it fell from Wither's tobacco-stained lips.

Tonight, I can go to sleep feeling like I've arrived at a place far from the reach of Jim Crow, where folks have nice homes, cars, jobs, and opportunity. I feel like I've found heaven on earth.

25

FAME CHURCH STORY

Sunday morning burst into the window at 5:00 a.m. The sun rises early this far north, and the birds are already making a ruckus. I find clean towels waiting in the bathroom, along with a hamper for my travel-worn clothes and a fresh bar of soap. By the time I step out of the shower, the steam is so thick, I figure I'll have to let it clear before I can shave.

When I enter the kitchen, Uncle Cecil is sitting at the table, sipping a cup of coffee and reading the *Seattle Post Intelligencer*.

"Hey, Junebug, how are you doing this morning? You're just in time for breakfast."

"Mmm, it smells good. Anything interesting in the paper?"

"Looks like they still don't have any leads in the Edwin Pratt murder but are trying to pacify the activists by making plans for a community center. You can take the sports section."

"Wait . . . not until you come over and give me a hug," chimes Aunt Fran.

She is frying bacon, and I'm happy to sidle over and see if I can snatch a piece from the plate she is filling up with the crisp pieces.

"Good morning, Junebug Wilson!" She raises her cheek for a kiss at the same time she slaps my hand away from the bacon. "Glad to see you in your Sunday clothes. Today, you're going to meet your second family. Everybody at FAME has been looking forward to meeting you."

I've always understood that going to church is part of the deal. Ever since Mama died, I'd let the church-going part slip away. After the family moved to Vicksburg, I worked every Sunday at the KFC.

Here, I am reminded it is a big part of life, and I wasn't about to insult my family by trying to pretend I have something better to do.

After breakfast, I help Aunt Fran with the cleaning up while Uncle Cecil polishes the car. By mid-morning, the three of us are back in the Oldsmobile, headed to the First African Methodist Episcopal Church, or FAME, as it's called by the community.

Uncle Cecil finds a spot in a far corner of the parking lot.

"Cecil, that's too far. You better hope I don't scuff up these shoes walking across that gravel."

I find it interesting that Uncle Cecil is so worried about getting dings in the parking lot, given the way he routinely zips between cars in traffic.

Walking through the parking lot, dodging the ladies with their wide-brimmed hats and the folks loitering in groups saying howdy, is a lot like getting to the stadium at a Vicksburg football game. It is slow-going. Everything feels tight. My shoes, my suit jacket, and the tie Aunt Fran cinched up under my chin. I am intentional about looking friendly, even though I feel like a nervous mess. Trying to stay close, but not too close so as not to get separated from his new family, I continue to harbor mixed feelings about going to church.

Why do people explain bad things away by saying they are God's will?

Some bad memories about how so-called "good church people," who've been so mean spirited, gossiping, and passing judgment on how people live their lives, creep in. But then again, here I am in Seattle, living in a nice house and eating bacon for breakfast. That itself is almost a miracle. Daddy's sisters want to help me, and they all love their church. The least I can do is be a good sport and try to make them proud.

My feet are hurting and it's hard to take in a deep breath because of this tight jacket, but I follow Aunt Fran through the gregarious crowd, smiling and nodding and agreeing with the feeling that I am happy to be in Seattle and looking forward to joining the church.

No one prepared me for the size of the church. It covers most of a city block. As we walk up the front steps, we stop to visit with another throng of people who greet me and pat me on the back. It's getting close to noon, and the organ strikes the first chord. Apparently, that is a signal to get in your seat.

I follow Aunt Fran and Uncle Cecil up the aisle until they find their usual spot in the middle of the nave. We all crowd into the pew, and Aunt Fran passes me a hymnal.

The organ pauses; the choir stands and focuses their gaze on their leader. Then the church fills with their harmony. I feel awe-struck.

Early summer sunshine streams into the church, illuminating the stained-glass windows, sending beams across the congregation. Right then, emotion smacks me upside the head. Maybe God is at work after all. Is this how it feels, belonging in a community of welcome and acceptance? Finding my voice, I join in singing the entry hymn, thankful and determined to make my family proud.

> *The Lord my pasture shall prepare,*
> *and feed me with a shepherd's care:*
> *His presence shall my wants supply,*
> *And guide me with a watchful eye*
> *My noonday walks he shall attend,*
> *And all my midnight hours depend.*

The congregation's enthusiasm and the power of the music lift my spirits. The reverend stands before the congregation at the pulpit. He welcomes everyone, including the newcomers to the church and to a life that emulates Jesus Christ, our Savior.

Reverend Johnson begins another song. After the first line, he waits for the choir to respond with an answer. An elderly sister playing the piano makes my heart swell. I have never heard such a full choir and have never felt this way.

The song ends, and Reverent Johnson faces the congregation from the pulpit. "Today, we read the Scripture from Jesus's Sermon on the Mount. 'But I say to you that everyone who is angry with his brother will be liable to judgment; whoever insults his brother will be liable to the council; and whoever says, 'You fool!' will be liable to the hell of fire.' Brothers and Sisters, before Jesus came to Earth, God commanded, 'Do not kill.' Today, we are told not to judge, insult, or show anger. Jesus shows us in every story how to ask and pray for help and how to seek repentance. Before you get worried, and start thinking, 'How am I going to stop getting irritated with my brother or sister,' remember this commandment replaces all the others: 'Love your neighbor as yourself.' Focus on the love, and the anger will melt away . . ."

I've never heard words like that spoken in church. "Love one another and the anger will melt away . . ." Maybe that is something I can try, especially with feeling guilty about the times I've let my temper get the best of me—like the fight with Mr. Bobby, the anger toward Daddy, and the way I'd wanted to punch the man who spit on me. I was nervous about coming to church with the weight of those transgressions and fearful of hearing about punishments. Now, I understand that there might be another way to find peace. And that turns my heart into something like butter in this pew.

After the sermon, there is more singing. Then it's time for us newcomers to come up front and join the church. I wish I could disappear. Walking up and kneeling before hundreds of people seems like a cruel exhibition. When I feel Aunt Fran and Uncle Cecil nudge me in the ribs, I set aside my nerves, and follow the small procession to the front of the church. There, I kneel in the sacristy with the other newcomers. Reverend Johnson grabs my hand and says, "Welcome to the FAME family of Christian soldiers."

As the reverend greets each newcomer, his voice raises in an invitation to the group clustered before and to the congregation. "Do you accept the Lord Jesus Christ as your personal Savior?"

The Church answers in unison, "I do."

I am no longer a backslider—the individual that ducks and dives in isolation or hides and prays at home while watching Sunday football games. Everyone prays that Jesus and His Father accept them and forgives their transgressions.

"Stay with us while we all affirm our faith with a recitation of the Apostle's Creed."

"We believe in one God, Creator of Heaven and Earth . . ."

I don't remember the words and keep my head down, listening carefully.

At the end of the prayer, the Reverend gives us new members permission to return to our seats. I notice Aunt Fran is beaming, and Uncle Cecil presses his hand on my shoulder as I slide back into the pew.

Announcements follow. There is a Baptism ceremony next month, and they invite all newcomers to attend Bible study meetings so we can be ready to be reborn with the Lord. After the service, everyone is invited to coffee, served in the Welcome Hall. The choir sings another hymn as the ushers help the congregation exit, row by row.

I'm feeling mighty grateful we didn't stay long in the church basement. I need some fresh air. I'm also thankful that Aunt Fran gregariously chats freely with all the well-wishers so I don't have to say much.

Suddenly, the long trip catches up with me, and I long to lie down on the bed in my new bedroom and fall into a deep sleep.

> I slept for hours in broad daylight, even sleeping through Sunday dinner. Luckily, Aunt Fran set aside a plate for me. Yesterday, the family's welcome party and today, the church . . . I'm feeling support from all directions. I never knew what I was missing.
>
> I started reading my Baptism pamphlet. It says when you get baptized, you get dunked in the water to symbolize dying. You die and then you get lifted back up to be reborn as a Christian. I'm not sure what that means. Everybody at the church seems

sure that getting reborn brings eternal life and puts you on some kind of assembly line to Heaven. If that's the case, why is it so random? I'm pretty sure Robert got baptized, and so was Mama. Sounds like Daddy got baptized back before he went to war. Then I read something about how after you're baptized, if you mess up and start sinning, you go to the other place and suffer for eternity. How can I be sure that I won't make a mistake?

All the kind people who welcomed me and filled the church with prayer and song seemed happy and secure. Maybe this is what I need, a good dose of Christianity. I want to believe and be part of it all, but I'm confused and still have some doubts.

I found this quote in the pamphlet:

"Prayer is a conversation of the heart with God'
Prayer is simply enjoying God's presence throughout the day."

Maybe I can just focus on that for now.

26

BOEING

In my sound sleep, I'm dreaming. I'm on a blanket in a cool meadow, surrounded by birds, crickets, and Mama humming. The smell of bacon drifts on the air. A distant chopping or knocking grows louder. Maybe Daddy is chopping wood. Maybe it will be chilly tonight, and we'll have a fire. I feel warm and sink deeper into the soft bed. The chopping gets louder, then Aunt Fran appears, too energetic for this late at night. *It is a dream! This is Monday morning!*

"Junebug Wilson, wake up! There's a good breakfast waiting for you . . . and a bright new day filled with opportunity, but you've got to rise and shine before it passes you by!"

I bolt straight up, awake. "Yes, ma'am, Aunt Fran, I'll be right down."

"About time you heard me, boy. Put on your 'looking for a job' clothes because that's your job today. I'll see you in ten minutes."

I place my feet on the ground and stand up. Last night, Aunt Fran said, "This nice room will be yours for the future if you keep your nose clean." She didn't go into specifics at that moment, and I hope she never feels like she needs to. If she says I'm gonna go get a job today, I aim to believe her, and if she says to be ready to look for a job in ten minutes, I can't waste time.

Aunt Fran had set a neat table for breakfast. Uncle Cecil sits at his place, reading the *P.I.*, sipping from his cup of coffee. He looks up and hands me the Sports section, saying, "Good morning, Wilson."

Aunt Fran brings me a plate filled with bacon, eggs, and toast. Then she sets down a nice dish of raspberry jam. "Aunt Mary makes this every year from the berries she grows in her backyard." She gets to telling me about when she worked at Boeing during the war. "I was who they call, 'Rosie the Riveter.' We women kept the air force supplied with jets and helped win the war. Those were the days! Hard work, but I liked the pay, and it felt good to be doing my part. Now I work at the Seattle Opportunity Industrial Center, or SOIC for short. It's near the Pratt Center We work with companies to find jobs for folks who need a little help to make the right connections."

Uncle Cecil looks up from the paper. "Wilson, remember yesterday, some of us were talking about Edwin Pratt and all the work he did to bring the civil rights movement to Seattle? The sad part, and I guess you could also say the important part of it, is that after his assassination, people finally started paying attention to his work."

Aunt Fran jumps in. "Now Cecil, don't get all intellectual on us. The simple fact is that at the Pratt Center, you can fill out an application and talk to some good people who will help you get a job at Boeing."

I've heard many people talk about Boeing, a place where it seems like almost everyone knows someone who works there. That was all I knew about it, though—other than they make airplanes.

I'm not too sure why they would hire me, but I suppose it won't hurt to try, and if it means keeping my nose clean, I'll do whatever Aunt Fran tells me to do.

"Yes, ma'am. I'll get over there as soon as I can. But what if I get lost?"

"Junebug Wilson, of course you'll get lost, and then you'll get unlost. Just remember to take the bus to town on the right side of the street and come home taking the bus on the left side. Ask for help if you get lost. It will all work out, and you'll get a good-paying job that will help when you go to the U of W this fall."

The bottom drops out of my stomach. *U of W? I thought I was going to Seattle Central Community College.* But for the sake of Aunt Francis and my need to focus on one thing at a time, I smile and head for the door.

"Wait!" she calls out, then hands me three crisp dollar bills and two quarters. "That's for bus fare and lunch. There's a lunch counter at the Woolworths two blocks from the Pratt Center where you can get a sandwich and a coke. Now, give me a hug and get on your way."

The number 43 slides up to the bus stop. The driver is friendly and tells me to sit up near the front and listen out for "Broadway and Pine."

"The Pratt Center will be in the Oddfellows Building, across the street."

The ride gives me another opportunity to see the city. I take note as the bus fills up with people on their way to work. Many of the passengers must have been riding the same bus every day for years the way they greet each other like old friends. The bus heads north on Broadway, and I ask the lady sitting beside me to tell me when we get close to Pine.

"That's one stop after mine. You'll hear the driver call it out, and there's a gang of folks who get off there too. Don't worry, you won't miss your stop. Where are you going on Pine?"

I told her about applying for a job at Boeing.

She has a kind face and bright eyes. "That will be really good if you get on there."

She turns around and gets the attention of the man holding his lunch box behind us. "Sammy, you get off on Pine. This young man is looking for the Edwin Pratt office in the Oddfellows Building. Do you think you can help him?"

"That's on my way to where I work. Son, walk with me, and I'll show you right where it's at."

My grasshoppers settle down as I look out the window and enjoy the blooming trees and fresh sea air that swoosh into the bus every time the door opens.

The Edwin Pratt Center is in an office on the first floor. In front of the door, I hesitate. The office is smaller than I expected. A counter takes up most of the space. Behind the counter are two women, typing at small tables. A man stands at the counter and talks on the telephone. And an old Formica lunch table, surrounded with four folding chairs, blocks the space between the door and the counter. Somehow, I dodge the table and walk up to the counter.

The man on the phone nods, holding up a finger to let me know he'd just be another minute.

When he hangs up the phone, he says, "Good morning. How can I help you?"

"My name is Wilson Reed Jr.," and I explain about Aunt Francis sending me down to apply for a job.

"I'm Sam McCoy. I'm glad to meet you, Wilson. You say your Aunt Francis sent you to this office. Is her last name Saunders?"

"Yes, sir. She works for the SOIC and is always on the lookout for opportunities."

"Oh, yes. I know Mrs. Saunders. She helps many people around here. Well, young man, you came to the right place. I've got an application. You can take it with you or fill it out right here."

"Thank you. I'd like to fill it out here and now, if you don't mind."

Sam nods, "Of course. The only thing is, you'll need to list three references. One could be your aunt or uncle. It would be good to have two who have standing in the community. Will you need to go home to get those?"

"No, sir. I have business cards for Reverend Johnson and Mr. Evans right here in my pocket."

"Well then, you can sit at the table and fill out the paperwork. Do you need a pen?"

"No, sir. I have a pen in my pocket."

"Mr. Wilson, I'm impressed with how well you come prepared. You'd be surprised how many people don't think about having references, let alone a pen, when they go to look for a job. I see a bright future for you."

I don't ever remember a man behind a counter suggesting I might have a bright future, and I tell him so. We enjoy a good chuckle, then I take the application and sit down.

By the time I've filled it out and double-checked to make sure everything is right, hunger pangs start moaning.

Aunt Fran's money is enough to get a sandwich and coke, just like she promised, plus there's still enough bus fare to get home. I wish I could tell her I had a job for sure. Sam told me he'd find out in two or three weeks.

"But don't worry. You meet the qualifications."

I don't know how. I am unemployed and poor.

Today was my first time riding a city bus in Seattle. I was nervous but the bus driver helped let me know my stop, and people were friendly. Seems like many people who ride the bus become friends. Aunt Fran was right. I could get to the Pratt Center, fill out my application, and get home before one o'clock. It seemed like a strange place to go to get a job at a big, modern corporation. They had slapped together the office pretty fast. The furniture was old and cheap—also the people who worked there didn't seem to have been doing that job for very long. I wonder what kind of job they are giving out to "poor, unemployed" young men, and what that has to do with riots and Edwin Pratt.

At dinner tonight, I asked Uncle Cecil to tell me more about the man, Edwin Pratt. He explained that Edwin Pratt was a Seattle Civil Rights leader who was the executive director of the Seattle Urban League. He had moved to Shoreline, a suburb just north of Seattle and joined a church to integrate the suburbs. The Urban League staff multiplied from four to twenty-seven individuals during his tenure.

They assassinated him on the doorstep of his Shoreline, Washington, home, with his wife and children inside, on a dark night in January 1969. He was only thirty-nine.

Now I understand why the Church and business people got busy implementing affirmative action and a summer program to keep Black males off the streets in Seattle.

Maybe I shouldn't look a gift horse in the mouth, but something seems very temporary about this situation. It's still an opportunity that I plan to take advantage of soon.

———

UNIVERSITY OF WASHINGTON

1969

27

COLLEGE

JUNE 8, 1969

The next day is Tuesday. I get up early, get dressed, and I'm at the breakfast table before Aunt Fran has to think about waking me. By the time I eat breakfast, I've received an update on the world news from Uncle Cecil, read the Sports section, accepted a new assignment from Aunt Fran, and received another three dollars, which I slide into my pocket.

While walking toward the door, the phone rings. Aunt Fran calls out, "Junebug Wilson, wait. Mary has some news. Cecil, find Section B, page two in the newspaper." I meander into the kitchen and Uncle Cecil has the article spread open so we can all read it.

Aunt Fran hangs up the phone and grabs my arm. "This is great news! Remember yesterday, I told you that you'd be applying at the University of Washington? That was my plan, but I wasn't sure how it was going to work. Mary saw this in the paper and called to tell us about it. Cecil, here's the scissors. Please cut out the article."

The article explains how the university is starting a special program to help students from under-represented minority groups attend the school and work toward earning a degree. This opportunity came about because of a protest. I immediately think of Jerry.

We read about how last spring, a group of activists had organized a sit-in at the office of the college president and refused to leave until he promised to create a program that would increase diversity in the student body. That was the birth of the Equal Opportunity Program that was now opening up educational opportunities, and I somehow am in the right place at the right time to grab a hold of the chance to get a college degree in a highly regarded university. All the information I need to get started is in the article.

Aunt Fran doesn't mince words. "Junebug, the Lord has listened to our prayers. He got you here safe and sound. Now He's showing you how you can make something of yourself. Get over to that university and let them know you are smart, a good learner, and ready to work hard to earn a degree. Go on now, we can't wait to hear all about it at dinner." She shoos me out the door.

I hit the ground running, huffing and puffing to catch the Metro, number forty-three. I'm relieved and happy to see the same driver as yesterday, who greets me warmly.

"Hello, young man. I'm glad to see you back again this morning. Where are you going today?"

He seems to me he's genuinely interested in helping. He hands me a schedule to help me get to and from the University District.

Most of the same passengers are on the bus, and they, too, are all friendly. Everyone wants to help me, and honestly, that's a bit confusing. *Maybe, I have an invisible sign on my forehead that says, "Country hick from French lick, Mississippi."*

Questions fly at me from every direction, and I'm not unlike a fish in a bowl. "Thank y'all for asking. Let me try to answer one at a time: I'm from Vicksburg, Mississippi; I got here last Saturday; I'm staying with family who moved up here sixteen years ago; my plans are to get a job and enroll in college, and today, I'm headed to Schmitz Hall to apply for a program that starts in the fall."

It feels good to get a round of "Way to gos!" and slaps on my back. I've never experienced bus rides like this, certainly not in Vicksburg, and it is a far cry from what I experienced in Detroit in 1967.

The bus follows the same route as yesterday, but today, I have to transfer to the bus that goes to UW. I'm surprised to realize I'm not feeling any grasshoppers. I guess it's because the bus driver explained exactly what I need to do, and he seems confident that if I needed more help, I would get it.

Once the bus nears downtown, the regulars get off at their stops, and new passengers step on. Not long after the aisle seat beside me opens up, a lady sits down. "Hello. I'm Mary."

I hold out my hand and reply, "Nice to meet you, Mary. I'm Wilson." Of course, I'm still using my given name to sound proper.

With a broad smile, she says, "I detect a Southern accent. Where are you from?"

Before I can answer, she continues, "Bigfoot country or down under, right?"

On that chilly summer morning, I quickly realize I am the butt of a Seattle-style joke. Mary is not condescending; she is "forward and funny." I'd never been told I have an accent before this. I guess I'm just a country boy with a Southern accent who has lived his whole brief life in Mississippi. I suppose everyone has some kind of accent.

Mary is kind but not Southern or folksy. And she is a wealth of information. So much so, I take notes in my little black journal, which is already full of information from my Greyhound bus trip.

"Mary, my folks shared an article with me about a new program at the University for poor folks trying to get a jump start on a college education."

"I work on the street near campus and can point you in the right direction. Get off with me at my stop. Schmitz Hall is just a short walk from the bus stop."

That is good news to these ears. I look out the window at my new city, Seattle, with all the hills and valleys covered with beautiful trees and shrubbery. Seattle is still a foreign country for this eighteen-year-old kid from Vicksburg, who is turning nineteen soon. July 2nd. That's my birthday, and it's coming up real quick.

As the bus makes the turn past the Montlake Bridge, I sense we're entering the "Husky Dawg" community. Purple and gold UW signs are everywhere. The University of Washington students, staff, and faculty sure are a proud bunch, according to Mary Bowman, a lifelong Seattleite and twenty-year member of the Fine Arts department on campus, so she tells me.

Mary wishes me luck and leaves me with some powerful observations and insights. "First, you are a million miles from Mississippi. People are nice here in the area. However, they will not invite you to dinner." She adds, "Some of us call it the *illusion of inclusion*."

A motley crowd exit the bus with us at the major stop for the university campus. I have never seen such a diverse group of people crowded together in one place. Asian students and businessmen; young people with patched jeans, flowing peasant dresses and long hair, and professorial types, wearing worn sport coats and soft-soled shoes shuffle on and off the bus. I stick close to my newest friend, Miss Mary.

Once grounded, we step back from the crowd, waiting for the crosswalk light to change. Mary points me toward my destination and makes sure I spot the boxy gray building that houses the student admissions office.

She says, "I look forward to seeing you around on campus, and maybe on the bus." Then she gives me her business card.

"Call me if you find yourself in a jam in the future."

"Thanks, Mary." I am feeling grateful to have met such a kind lady.

Schmitz Hall is busy. Students are standing in lines or milling around the edges of the hallways and lobby. The grasshoppers churn; I just don't like to make mistakes and getting lost is one of my greatest fears, right up there with the fear of being laughed at. My chances of falling victim to at least one of those fears today feels about as high as finding a French racoon in Redwood Mississippi. *Dude, you need a sack of courage—ASAP*, I whisper to myself. This nearly makes me laugh, and I realize my stomach has settled down. Aunt Mary had told me, "When you get nervous, call on the Lord, say these words to yourself, 'The Lord is with me; I will not be afraid,' then take a breath and look for a sign." I follow her advice at this very time.

Feeling calmer—don't you know it—I scan the lobby and see a sign. "Office of Minority Affairs, 3rd Floor." I find the stairs and climb up to the third landing, where I see the office right in front of where I'm standing.

Inside, I see another sign. "Information." The receptionist tells me to please wait until Tammy can see me, so I find a chair.

Tammy Mudge enters and greets me with a warm handshake and a grin. "Follow me down the hall to the EOP office."

Next, I meet Tom Felder, a tall man wearing a khaki suit.

"Tom can help you get your application started," explains Tammy. "I'll bet you could use a cup of water." That's when I suddenly realize I am thirsty and gladly accept the offer.

The water, too, helps calm the hopping critters in my belly.

Tom launches into an explanation of the new Educational Opportunity Program. He explains how his office has been working to spread the word throughout the state and has even been reaching out across the US, including the South. He seems proud that they've had a trickle of students arrive from the South, including two other men from Jackson, Mississippi in the last two days.

I learn they designed the program to provide "nontraditional" students with support, to help them earn a college degree from an esteemed university.

The term, *nontraditional*, confuses me. And I wonder how I might qualify with a 2.3 GPA from Utica Community College. Tom explains the EOP promotes academic success and graduation for under-represented ethnic minorities and first-generation college students at the University of Washington.

"I'm going to ask three questions to find out if you meet the qualifications. Would you be the first person in your generation to earn a four-year degree?"

"Yes, sir."

"Is your family's income below the national poverty level?"

"Yes, sir."

"Did you attend segregated schools in Mississippi?"

"Yes, sir, I did."

"Well," says Tom, "Let's get you started filling out the paperwork. Do you have questions?"

"Just one, sir. Can I fill out the application here in the office, or do I have to take it home and mail it?"

Tom suggests I complete the application in the office and try to call my old schools to get my records. That isn't easy—at all. But I get it done.

After spending the day cooped up in a stuffy office, squinting at tiny boxes and narrow lines, it feels good to step outside into a new world. The clouds and haze are gone, replaced by bright sunlight and blue skies. Schmitz Hall is on University Avenue, off campus, and inspiration fueled by simply having my feet on the actual campus where I hope to be a student this fall propels me.

I walk up a short flight of stairs and follow a path that cuts through a row of hedges. It opens to an area surrounded by stately brick buildings with leaded glass windows and heavy timber doors. More walkways spread out to more buildings. Somewhere, I hear a fountain and realize I am on the edge of a giant campus that's even bigger than all of Vicksburg, Mississippi.

But now, I need to find my way back home to the south end, retracing my steps back to the bus stop that was opposite the one where Mary and me had disembarked this morning.

I'll have to transfer downtown to the bus I take to get home. It would be awful to get on the wrong bus and get taken off in the opposite direction. Worry stirs the grasshoppers inside.

Thankfully, it only takes a minute to find a friendly face.

I catch the eye of a well-dressed young man who knows how to get down to the south end and he tells me to take the seven downtown and the thirty-two to Lake Ridge. He is a former UW student, now working in the Safeco building on the corner of 43rd and Brooklyn.

"I'm taking the seven downtown and then transferring to the eigh-teen. You can ride with me downtown, and I'll show you where to catch the thirty-two."

The seven pulls up within a few minutes, and I follow my new friend up the stairs. The bus is so crowded that we're lucky to find a place to stand together and continue our conversation. I grab a firm hold of the rod attached to the ceiling and flex my knees, careful to keep my balance as the bus jerks forward.

My new acquaintance asks, "What's your name?"

"Wilson Edward Reed Jr. is my formal name, but all my friends and family call me Junebug."

"I'm Ray Johnson." Ray wants to know where "Junebug" was from and how long I've been in Seattle.

"I just got off the boat, or rather Greyhound, from Mississippi on Saturday." My grin gives away my joke.

"Welcome! That's a long way to ride on a bus. We might be kin folk because I'm also from the South. From now on, I'm calling you Home-town, if you don't mind. New city, new name."

I laugh, and it feels good. "Just don't call me late for dinner."

In less than half an hour, it seems we've hit it off like we'd been friends forever. Ray is kind and forthright. "Man, I'm glad we met. I feel like we've been friends for years," I admit to Ray.

"Me too, Hometown."

The long bus ride gives me a chance to ask Ray about the university. I'm hoping for an unvarnished view of the University of Washington. "What is the general image of the university in the larger community?"

"It depends who you're talking to in the community. Some educated folks with degrees from Seattle love the place. Some others think the UW takes a lot and does not give back to the local community enough."

"Do you think the new EOP/Minority Affairs Program is genuine in its intentions, Ray?"

Ray pulls his head back and widens his eyes. "I don't know how to answer. Hmm, that's a big question to ask a guy trying to hang on without falling into that nice lady's lap." He winks at the elderly lady sitting directly in front of his knees.

Then he's quiet for a moment before saying, "If I was you, I would take full advantage of the new programs to the hilt. Get involved with the academics and do not look back buddy."

After another pause, he adds, "The UDub is big business. Old rich men and families protect the U and resist change. The frats and sororities control social life. Big money comes from football tickets and games."

We are quiet again for a few minutes while people jostle past us. Number seven travels downtown along Fourth Avenue, letting five to ten people on and off at each stop. We continue adjusting to the every-changing crowd. Then the bus driver announces, "Westlake!"

"This is where we get off."

Once on the ground, Ray explains, "Your bus should come along pretty soon. Wait here, jump on the thirty-two, and you'll be home in a half hour."

We hit each other five and do a bear hug. "You can call me at work. Here's my card. Take care, Hometown."

Ray was right. I am home in less than thirty minutes.

Aunt Fran and Aunt Mary are waiting for me. They both scream, "Welcome home, College Boy!" when I walk through the door. "Sit down and tell us all about your day." Aunt Fran points to the big armchair, and she and Aunt Mary perch on the couch, staring at me, with their hands clasped in their laps expectantly.

I see them smiling and nodding the whole time I tell them about meeting the people at EOP and filling out the paperwork. I tell them about Tom and Tammy and what I learned about the support and opportunities the program provides for "underrepresented students."

They seem more excited than I am when I tell them that if accepted, I would attend a two-day orientation, visit the Ethnic Cultural Center, and attend the tutoring program workshops and a luncheon. Also, if I qualify in a drawing or lottery, I might win two free tickets to attend the homecoming game against Michigan State in September.

Aunt Mary and Aunt Francis are cheerleaders, exclaiming their support and high expectations. Their praise and encouragement hit me like a shot of confidence, but deep down in my stomach, I feel a familiar stirring. *What if I don't make it?*

> Today was one for the record books. I've got a shot at going to the University of Washington. I never dreamed such a thing would ever be possible. Maybe, if I had, I would have worked harder on my grades. I learned how to work with my hands at the KFC, but school was easy enough for me to slide along without having to study. Now I'll have to learn how to use my brains—fast.
>
> People at the Equal Opportunity Office in the Schmitz Hall building told me all about the program and said I have a good chance to get in. They told me about how the Civil Rights Movement came to the university, about how the sit-in and Edwin Pratt's murder got politicians thinking that they needed to spread out the opportunities to minority students. They told me that because I would be the first person in my family to earn a college degree, because I grew up dirt poor, and because I've worked hard to rise up, I have a good chance.
>
> My Seattle family is excited, and I want them to be proud of me. But what about my Mississippi family? What opportunities are coming to my sisters? Melvin's still stuck working at the KFC and hasn't even graduated from high school . . . and Robert Scott came home in a coffin after serving his country in a foreign country's war.
>
> I guess I just need to keep doing like Aunt Fran and Aunt Mary say: get up early and go out and find two opportunities every day.

28

RIVETER HELPER

I figure my second visit to the Edwin Pratt makeshift office is going to be all business. I head back after a call and a letter to Aunt Fran's place in Lake Ridge. Aunt Fran and Uncle Cecil are still my cheerleading squad, and this morning, they're saying in unison, "You're going to do great in the interview and woo those people."

I now feel like a veteran bus rider in Seattle. I get to my ten o'clock appointment on time. I'd learned from my dad at an early age that the "early bird gets the worm." Dad seems to have been right about being prompt and on time. The folks at the front desk at the Pratt Center are kind and invite me to Room 101 for my Boeing interview.

Three representatives sit in folding chairs at one of those lunchroom tables. They seem a little out-of-place sitting on rickety old chairs in their good suits, but they are polite. All three rise to greet me and invite me to sit down with them. They introduce themselves. Mr. Anderson, who seems to me to be in charge, speaks first.

"Mr. Reed, may I call you Wilson?"

I speak up right away, "Yes, sir. Wilson is just fine."

"Wilson," he continues, "we're impressed with your application and wanted the chance to make your acquaintance. Although this is an entry-level job, you understand, any job at Boeing requires an employee who is very trustworthy and ready to become part of a structured team. We build aircraft that people all over the world trust to take them wherever they want to go . . . through all kinds of weather. We take the hiring process seriously. Before we make our final decisions, we want to meet each of the finalists to help us get a feel of their character and interest in becoming part of our team. We have two questions for you."

I nod and wait, unnerved to say anything just yet. Mr. Anderson shows nice manners, explaining why they have asked me to come back to the Pratt Center. I appreciate that. Mr. Andrews, the man sitting to the right of Mr. Anderson, asks the first question.

"First, who are you, Wilson Edward Reed?"

"I recently arrived in Seattle via Greyhound bus. I grew up outside of Vicksburg, Mississippi, raised on a rural family-owned farm in a small community called Redwood. I'm no stranger to hard work. As a little kid, I started working on the farm, pulling corn, hoeing cotton, and picking it in the early fall. My extended family lives here in Seattle. Aunt Fran and her husband Cecil are my immediate family that I live with for the summer. If I get this important job, Uncle Cecil will give me rides to the Renton Boeing industrial site and factory. I recently applied to attend UW this fall too. I'm happy to have this opportunity to share my background with each of you this morning and promise that if you hire me, you won't be sorry."

Maybe if they know I have a ride every day, I'll have an advantage over the other applicants.

Mr. Andrews says, "Thank you, Wilson. This would be quite a change from picking cotton."

The man to the left of Mr. Anderson is Mr. Sloan. He asks the second question. "Why should we hire you for the summer program?"

I take a breath and launch into an answer I hope will make Mrs. Watson proud:

"You should hire me because I am qualified and an extremely hard worker. My number one trait and characteristic is I pay attention to details, and secondly, I follow instructions from my supervisor. Furthermore, I show up daily and on time. My mother died when I was fourteen years old. After we moved to the city of Vicksburg, when I started high school, I held a steady job at the KFC, went to school, and helped take care of my little sisters. My daddy was a marine in World War II, and my mama worked as a housekeeper while taking care of us and working on the farm. I grew up in a family of doers. If you hire me, you will find me to be reliable, kind, and considerate of others' space and time. Finally, I am a mature team player."

When I stop, no one speaks for a few moments.

Finally, Mr. Anderson says, "Thank you, Wilson. It is a pleasure meeting you."

The three men stand, so I rise too. Each of them offers me his hand, which I gladly shake. *At least I know how to give a good handshake.*

In parting, Mr. Anderson says, "Wilson, you impress me as a young man who is working hard to get ahead. And you also seem like you will work for your team. We will let you know our decision within a week."

———

One week later, I receive a telephone call and an official letter that makes my heart swell a couple sizes. The Renton Boeing folks are hiring me for eleven weeks. Aunt Fran is so excited that she plans a celebration. That Sunday, all the family folks come over after church and the hoopin' and hollerin' begins. "Praise the Lord," says Aunt Mary.

I hear, "Prayers go up, blessings come down," repeated like a refrain throughout the house. And I can't find a quiet spot, away from the "amens and hallelujahs." Best of all, everyone brings something good to eat and the dining room table groans under the weight of casseroles and pies.

The other good news is I can start right after the Fourth of July holiday. They give me instructions for the clothes and equipment I need to be safe in the factory and on the assembly line. That means I have to purchase work pants, work shirts, and steel-toed boots. The company will supply a hard hat. The schedule is simple: Show up at work daily at 8:00 a.m.

Lunch is at noon for thirty minutes, and I get two fifteen-minute breaks, one in the morning and one in the afternoon. The day ends at 4:00 p.m. I just can't wait.

———————

The morning of my first day starts out like most, except Aunt Fran surprises me with Uncle Cecil's old lunch box. "Bag lunches have a way of getting smashed," she says by way of explanation.

When we drive up to where people can get dropped off, Uncle Cecil pats my shoulder. "You'll do just fine. We're all proud of you for landing this job."

"Thanks, Uncle Cecil. I'll do my best."

Inside, they send me to a room where there are already a few of my fellow employees sitting. At eight o'clock sharp, the supervisor, Mr. Germane, a no nonsense type, starts explaining the job. I quickly understand this man is focused on the rules and regulations that govern the plane assembly environment and production areas. He says, in no uncertain terms, that safety is number one. I listen while Mr. Germane explains the duties and responsibilities of the riveter helper job. In a nutshell, each of us should always follow the lead riveter instructions, listen carefully to each job duty and assignment, and watch our movements up and down the ladder to the plane and the area where we'll be working. I am glad to learn the bathroom and breakroom are close by. Besides for safety, none of us can leave the area they call "the pit" during the workday. Security badges are to be worn on the job. "They are apple red," says Germane.

After lunch on that first day, I understood what Mr. Germane meant about the bathroom. It is the biggest restroom I have ever seen—there were at least fifty stalls!

The new job feels mighty good. I don't mind the structured environment and the endless details. Before today, I'd only seen a plane in the air. By the end of the day, I decide that working as a riveter helper during the summer of 1969 is cool.

By the time I begin my second week, I realize I enjoy working and earning money much more than looking for work and depending on Aunt Fran to know when I need some cash. She is still making me lunches and buying extra treats to pack with my sandwiches. I make a plan to check out the local KFC to see if I can take on an extra job so I'm not eating all of her groceries, and I figure I can kick in some gas money.

The breakroom is the one place we can let down a little. I think of it as the nonsense environment, as opposed to the no-nonsense environment of the pit. I meet two jokers, Bernard Taylor and Lee Rawls, during lunch one day. I remember seeing them the first day, but after we got our assignments, the riveter helpers scattered throughout the enormous building and only see each other at lunch. Bernard and Lee talk non-stop about three things: cars, girls, and how they are going to spend the big paycheck they are earning in ten more weeks.

Bernard says, "I am going to buy myself a Cadillac and party like it's New Year's Eve."

I cannot believe my ears.

Lee, not to be outdone, says, "I am going to buy myself a sleek TR6 race car and go out to Long acres for the Labor Day weekend party."

"What are you going to do with your big paycheck in ten weeks, Junebug?" asked Bernard.

"I'm going to college at UW and major in history."

Their jaws drop. They look at each other, laugh, and shrug their shoulders. Then Lee pipes up again. "Square root and totally corny. Not hip."

"I am not taking you to any party with me, buddy. No girl is going to hang out with you."

I have just become persona non grata with his two workplace friends. They are no longer interested in hanging out with me. And that's fine by me too.

I just focus on what I can do—succeed at my job. I start humming and thinking. *I am not a dancer or a party dude, and I like my job at Boeing.*

I guess moving forward, I'll be a party pooper and a bookworm, and that's OK.

I fall into the daily routine at Boeing with ease. It brings order to my life. And I don't have any conflicts with the lead guy or my supervisor. Everything with being a male Rosie the Riveter is all right with me. According to Aunt Fran, Rosie kept her head down and did her job during World War II—an honorable job.

I imagine the jets flying into the clouds, heading to China. How would it feel to be buckled into a seat as the engines roar and the plane lifts into the air? I think I will have a blast the first time I g*et up in the friendly skies of United Airlines,* as they sing in the commercials.

Before working at Boeing, the only schooling I'd had about airplanes was a fifteen-minute segment back in the fourth grade about Orville and Wilbert Wright.

And look. Now I am working amid construction, smack in the action of building airplanes. I like the teamwork of building something important, where doing a good job matters and feel proud to look out and see at least ten planes and one hundred men working to get them up and flying, knowing that people from all over the world will travel in them.

Ten weeks later, I grab my journal.

I liked my eleven-week experience at Boeing as a riveter helper.

I smiled inside and thought, Edwin Pratt would be proud of the program started in his name. Me and a group of other young men got experience building airplanes, working as a team, earning good money and staying out of trouble during the Summer of 1969. Edwin Pratt was a friend of Dr. Martin Luther King. They both graduated from the same university. This program wasn't enough to end inequality, but it was an opportunity, and I learned things about work and industry that I couldn't have learned anywhere else.

Before starting at Boeing, I only knew how to work on the farm and fry chicken. Boeing gave me a chance to learn more about what a good job can do for a man and what a man can contribute to a company.

This is what I learned at Boeing:

- A successful employer treats everyone with respect.
- Bosses do not have to scream at employees to achieve results.
- An employer can protect employees from mayhem in the workplace.
- A successful employer makes sure everyone follows safety rules.
- Good teamwork benefits everybody.
- I am a good teammate in an organized structure that is results-oriented.
- I can work with others to achieve testable and measurable results daily.

My experience as a cook at KFC was unsafe. Back there, we all knew the rule was "protect yourself." I still have the scars from burns and scratches that have long since healed. The first thing I learned at Boeing was that safety is #1. In my old job at the KFC, we never thought about protecting ourselves from the boiling oil.

Now airplanes fascinate me even though I've never flown on one. I enjoyed working on something I had seen on TV. I also learned that I had a step up because many of the guys hired with me had little or no work experience.

Working as a man at Boeing, in a job like Aunt Fran's, helping to put jet airplanes together, made me think more about family. I keep wondering about Daddy. Did he fly on any airplanes in the war? Would he have liked a job like the one I had at Boeing? What opportunities did he have and what opportunities did he let pass him by? Does he ever think of me?

I'd like to talk to him . . . I heard from Bernice that he's going to visit in December. Maybe I could buy a ticket and fly there to be with them. Maybe we could mend some fences.

29

END OF SUMMER

The last Sunday in August is a special day. Aunt Fran has planned a surprise for Uncle Cecil's birthday, and I'm attending church again with the family. Ever since I started my second job, I haven't been able to attend Sunday service. Earning extra cash for school and giving my family a little relief from having to feed and support me just feels right, but I've missed church. This week, I told the manager I needed Sunday off, and luckily, I got it. But I know I'll have to quit soon. The manager will be sad to see me go because I am good in the kitchen, and the place has never run so smoothly. At least, that's what I hear.

At church, it feels like I've never even been away. I join in the songs and prayers, grateful for the company and community.

After the service, we go down for coffee. I didn't realize how festive they could make the old basement. Right up front, a six-foot table is set for a birthday celebration, and there's a big sheet cake, decorated with purple roses and "Happy Birthday, Cecil" in orange writing. A punch bowl with fancy cups stands ready beside the cake, with paper plates, plastic forks, and napkins fanned out in front of the cake. The special knife and pointed spatula sit ready for the cake cutting. All is ready for the guests. A sheet of butcher paper covers every table, and each is topped with a beautiful arrangement of prized dahlias from Aunt Fran's garden. The church ladies had arranged her red and pink pom-poms, cactus blooms with spiky purple and pink petals, and the delicate paper-thin single blooms in tall vases, low dishes, and mason jars. The blooms she's been babying all summer fill the basement.

When he sees the hubbub, Cecil gives Aunt Francis a stern look. She meets his eyes until they both start to laugh.

"Didn't I tell you I didn't want a fuss made for my birthday?"

"No, what I heard you say was that you'd be happy with a cup of coffee in the church basement. You're not complaining that you're getting a piece of cake to go with it are you?"

He narrows his eyes. "No, I'm OK with cake, but you know I don't like a lot of fuss."

A crowd is gathering around the table. Church ladies add spoonfuls of green sherbet to the punch, and my mouth waters.

Cecil puts on a good show of acting surprised. The entire congregation join in to sing "Happy Birthday," while Cecil waits stoically for his piece of cake. He is a loved and respected member of long standing, and the church loves its celebrations. The family keeps busy chatting with well-wishers.

I visit with many of them as they wait for their turn to congratulate Uncle Cecil and wish him many more trips around the sun. One person who greets me is Mr. Evans.

"Good to see you, Wilson. I hear you got on at Boeing. Good thing you had my card; I want you to know that I gave you a glowing recommendation. I told them that hiring you would be the best decision they'd make all year! How did it work out?"

"Thank you, sir. Yes, I sure appreciate your recommendation. I got to help the riveters. Just being inside a building that big was an adventure. It's so big it has its own climate. I never imagined how much space you need to be to build a passenger jet."

"Wilson, a lot of good people worked with Boeing executives to get them to create that program. Reverend Johnson wrote a letter and met with some top Boeing officials. A big corporation like that needs to employ people from the entire area, not just those who live in the north end. Do you think they'll hire you to work there next summer?"

"Maybe. I don't know what they're planning. I'm not sure if they know, either. It was a nice steady job, a good paycheck, and thanks to Uncle Cecil, I had a ride every day."

I really liked the job, but I wasn't expecting to have the same opportunity next summer. Management didn't give any sign one way or another that they are setting up a career path for disadvantaged young men. It seems more like they are offering the community a way to keep young men off of the streets during the summer. I figure Mr. Evans has been involved with getting the program started, so maybe he knows something.

Mr. Evans thumped me on the back. He is such a jovial man and someone who is good to have in your corner.

"Junebug, you may not realize it now, but for you to get that job was the final step in a long process."

All the time we've been talking, Mr. Evans has been glancing over toward Uncle Cecil. A space opens up, and he backs away from me, redirecting his attention and stepping away.

"Keep up the good work. You've got a bright future ahead of you!" By the time he finishes saying the last bit, he's already thrust his hand to Uncle Cecil.

I barely have time to take a bite of cake before Mrs. James nudges my elbow. She stands close enough to speak in a low voice, as if she is sharing a secret. "Wilson, I thought I should come and rescue you from you know who."

I am confused.

"You know his daughter is starting her senior year at Richmond Beach this year. She is a sweet girl. Have you met her?"

I take a bite of cake and step back.

"Don't worry, I won't tell anybody what you tell me. You'll be too busy going to school to think about girls, anyway, won't you?"

I figure you can find good gossip just about anywhere. And I know to keep my distance.

"Yes, ma'am. I'll be busy with schoolwork."

She whispers, "I know how happy your aunt is that you are living with her. It is so sad she never had children of her own." She looks at me and waits, staring up at my eyes with her face squished into a mask of concern.

Cousin Benny is standing close, so I say, "Excuse me," to Mrs. James, turn away, and engage with Benny.

"Hey, June, having fun yet? Tell me the real story about working at Boeing. Did you get to go up in any of those jets?" Cousin Benny always makes me laugh.

"Oh, man, you know all I did was stand on my feet all day while the riveter drilled screws to hold the covering on."

"Well, at least it kept you out of trouble and you made some money. Any chance you can get on full time?"

"Hardly. At the end, the supervisor gave a nice speech congratulating us and telling us how we could go back home and tell our people about our great experience. Then he asked us to tell him what job we'd want if we came back, and this guy, Lee, popped off, 'I want your job!' It was pretty much downhill from there."

I stop to let us both laugh.

"That put an end to the speech. He wished us well and left the scene. It seemed more like a program to prop up themselves in the eyes of the community than something they were using to make any actual change."

Reverend Johnson has a son, Johnny, a year ahead of me in school. Johnny is attending Seattle Community College with the plan to transfer to UW in his junior year. He walks up to me and Benny.

"Hey, Wilson, maybe one of these days we'll be sitting at the stadium. Good luck on getting in. You must be a lot further ahead in your studies than I am. I thought for sure my 3.20 GPA from Garfield would get me in. But I guess I didn't have your connections. Your aunts are surely good at figuring out the system."

Benny always has a good comeback. "Surprising that admissions didn't pay attention to all of your *A*s in PE and Home Ec., Johnny."

"I took my share of college prep, but you know I was busy helping my dad with his mission to Africa. It wasn't easy keeping my grades up."

I need some air. I look over at Aunt Fran. She and the helper ladies have cleared the tables and are washing the punch bowls. They have all the flowers distributed in jars for people to take home. People are filtering out through the doors, and it suddenly seems quiet.

If Johnny couldn't get in with a 3.20 GPA, how am I going to succeed? Johnny had gone to Garfield, a big city high school, while I went to a segregated small-town high school. Temple had produced many successful professionals, but it was still small. Utica was a trade school, with little emphasis on the skills you need to excel in Top 50 universities. Maybe this was all a pipedream, and I'm not ready at all. I'm feeling both exhausted and grateful that it's almost time to leave. So I start for the door.

Benny is helping Aunt Mary carry some flowers to the car. I call out to him. "Bye for now, Benny. I'll be able to go to church again regularly in September when I'm done at the KFC."

Benny says, "Hey, Junebug, wait a minute, I want to tell you something."

I pick up a load of flowers and follow him to the car.

At the Oldsmobile, Benny says, "Don't pay any mind to Johnny. With your energy and drive, you're going to do well at the U. You aren't afraid of hard work, and that's the most important thing. Remember what Thomas Edison said, 'Genius is 1 percent inspiration and 99 percent perspiration.' Hang in there, and you'll do fine. Don't worry about what anybody says."

"Thanks, Benny; you're beginning to sound like Aunt Fran. Please don't tell her that, or I'll be hearing it every morning when I wake up." *Maybe I need to tell myself that every morning.*

―――――

That night, I don't sleep well. Mostly because of a nightmare that I missed the bus to school. Then there is a nightmare that Mrs. James, Mr. Evans, and Johnny surround me on the bus, filling the air with their advice. I remember Thomas Edison's quote but worry hard work wouldn't be enough. *I'll write in my journal. Then I'll get some sleep.*

I've been thinking about today's readings and Rev. Johnson's sermon. Romans 12:3–13 had a lot to say about community.

I keep thinking about this one: "Be devoted to one another in love. Honor one another above yourselves."

He talked about how much more we can build when we all work together. He made it sound easy. I wonder if Daddy ever heard that one: "Honor one another above yourselves."

It was a rousing sermon, and I felt the pull, but it's hard to reconcile the words about love and forgiveness with the realities of selfish fathers and Jim Crow. I'm grateful to be here and count my blessings. But sometimes, it seems like I'm looking through a veil of promises in order to ignore the realities of injustice. I just can't seem to stay focused on the positive so that I can sleep.

Maybe I just got worked up because when Johnny started talking about how his GPA of 3.20 wasn't good enough, I started wondering why I thought I had a chance. Maybe Johnny just said those things because he's jealous. He doesn't know what it means to skip dinner because you only have enough food left for breakfast, and he's probably never had to use an outhouse, but whatever he thinks or feels, it's not my business.

I may have been disappointed by Daddy and Vicksburg, but I've been supported in many ways since moving to Seattle. I'm living in a world of opportunity and support, even if, at times, I'm disappointed.

Maybe that is enough for now. I'm getting sleepy.

30

COLLEGE BOY

"You are accepted into a giant fraternity of Husky Dawgs."

The acceptance call and letter from Tom means I am heading into the big times academically. I will not have to attend another segregated school for the rest of my life, unless he choose to on my own. This is a big deal.

I am feeling overly excited about my new station in life, and I even pinch myself as I remember the day I stepped foot on the campus for the first time. I was afraid to believe I could actually become a student here. Now, it is all coming true. My future is in my two hands for the first time in my life.

The best part is that my Seattle family is all aboard the Junebug train. Aunt Mary leads the chorus. "College boy from little Vicksburg makes it big! We are proud of you Junebug Wilson and your daddy and family down-home will be extra proud of you, son."

The phone rings non-stop. As soon as we finish getting congratulated from one church member, another calls. Everybody wants to share in the good news. Jubilation fills the house, to the point that I want a little time to myself. I'm still not used to so much attention and am ready to disappear to my room to read and maybe write in my journal.

Aunt Fran interrupts me in mid-step. "You can't go anywhere; you need to stay here and talk to these people. We support each other for the good of the whole, through thick and thin. That means when people are happy for you, you accept their good wishes, and when something important happens to them, you call and let them know you care."

That evening, the whole family gathers for dinner. Uncle Cecil leads the prayer, giving a special blessing for my success. At the end of the prayer, he adds, "We are proud beyond belief of the opportunity for Wilson Edward Reed Junior to finally benefit from his years of struggling to make something of himself."

Later, I find my time to write.

> It really happened. I'm a Husky. I'm on target to earn a college degree from one of the top fifty universities in the country. I'm done with segregated schools, where everything is handed-me-downs. I'll get to go to football games with brothers and white students, go to the concession stand, and sit wherever I want. I'm going to learn whatever I missed out on and make something out of myself. I just need to keep my head down and work hard.
>
> But what if I can't? Seems like those old worries just hang around the corner till I give them a chance to start creeping into my imagination. I don't want to disappoint anyone: the good folks down in Mississippi, my new Seattle family, my new professors, and especially, I don't want to disappoint all the folks that protested and risked being arrested to enroll "underrepresented students" like me. I can't let fear knock me off a good roll, so I'll just do my best.
>
> I can be happy right now. I'm not alone. I have family, a church community, and people at the EOP office ready to help. What a change from fearing for my life, jumping at every noise, seeing no future, to this. On Monday, I'm going to orientation, and I'm going to find out all I can about how to be successful.

31

THE ORIENTATION

On Monday, I find the HUB, or student union building. I'm early, but already, a big crowd is gathering. Purple and gold is everywhere. At 9:00 a.m., the 200 new students are called to attention. Vice President of Minority Affairs Dr. Sam Kelly welcomes everyone. I've heard he was a general, and Dr. Kelly addresses us with military authority. "You cannot go wrong in the EOP program. We have built a solid foundation for your success."

Next, Tammy and Tom say a few words about the EOP and introduce the esteemed panel. Each member repeats a different version of the same message. *Take advantage of this opportunity. The University of Washington embraces you, and we of the Equal Opportunity Program are here to help. Our doors are always open to each one of you.*

After the panel introduces themselves, Tom addresses the crowd once more.

"Thank you all for coming today. This is going to be an exceptional year for the Dawgs! Look around. You are looking at the first EOP class, the Class of 1972. We represent every corner of the United States and every economic background. Get to know each other and make friends. You are about to make lifelong friendships, and you are joining a community who will have your back.

"Tonight, we are looking forward to getting to know each other better. The EOP and Department of Minority Affairs are hosting a dinner and an after party. Make yourselves at home!"

After the meeting, I hang around, thinking this might be a good opportunity to meet my professors before classes start.

Dr. Trevor Chandler is shaking hands with students near the window that look out onto Lake Washington. I patiently wait until he can introduce himself.

The professor greets me and says, "Welcome, young man."

Dr. Chandler is a professor in the Political Science department at UW. "I have been where you are going. Keep your head up high, and do not let them see you blink. You rode the bus up here from Mississippi for 2,600 miles, so you can do anything, young man. Come and see me when you complete your BA degree. I like young people with energy, and you might be a good fit to work as my TA."

I simply can't think of how to answer. Dr. C. sees something in me that I just cannot see in myself, and again, that strange mixture of grasshoppers and pride churn in my belly.

"Thank you, sir. I'll do my best."

"Of course you will, Wilson. That's why we selected you."

After the orientation, I stroll around the campus before returning to Aunt Mary's. Even though I don't think of myself as a party dude, I know this is my last chance to meet my classmates, professors, and staff before the rush of the school year begins. I'll look my best and make a good impression, even though I'd rather spend the evening reflecting and going to bed early.

So I jump back on the bus by 5:30 p.m., arriving with plenty of time before the dinner starts.

When I enter Lander Hall, it's already filling up. The aromas of roasting meat and fresh-baked bread drift through the hall, reminding me of my hunger. I wonder, *Why are the EOP organizers so insistent that we all attend the dinner and the after party?* I think my top priority should be my studies so how is going to a party going to help with understanding any-thing about oceanography?

Lamar is hanging out with a couple of his LA buddies near the entrance. I join them. After a few minutes, the LA buddies wander off to visit with some girls, leaving me and Lamar to ourselves. I had originally told Lamar I didn't think I'd stay for the party.

"You got to show, brother," said Lamar. "If you fail to show, I will tell everyone that you are a square from Mississippi. At that point, everyone will laugh at you."

I was sure Lamar was putting on the ritz—jive-talking me into rolling over and saying yes. Lamar reminds me of one of my high school friends, Mark Taylor.

"Lamar, remember I came 2,600 miles to be a successful student. I didn't travel that far to be a party dude. Besides, I don't know how to dance. And I'm serious. Do not tell anyone."

Lamar let loose a belly laugh that went on longer than I thought nec-essary. "You gotta be joking, Ed Reed."

Lamar is the first friend to change my name at UW.

I soon discover everybody knows Lamar. He's a speaker at orientation, a U of W graduate, and third-year law student. He is from Compton, in Los Angeles, and has a real friendly, upbeat style. With Lamar at my side, I feel more at ease, especially when my new friend breaks the ice by introducing me as Ed Reed. Lamar reminds folks that several NFL players have the same name, which started some fun conversations about sports.

An announcement directs everyone to find their seats. Lamar leaves to find his spot with the EOP leaders, and I select a spot at a back table where I am soon joined by seatmates that look as new as me.

The man sitting on my right is about my height and busy examining his place setting and turning his glass of water in circles.

"Hi, I'm Ed. I came all the way from Mississippi." The simple fact seems like a good way to break the ice.

The young man meets my eyes. "Juan," he replies and gives me a firm handshake. "I came all the way from Yakima." He laughs because Yakima is in Washington, just across the mountains. "Compared to Mississippi, Yakima seems pretty close," he adds.

The man on my left laughs with us and says, "I'm Raymond, all the way from Tulalip."

"Ed, I don't know how well you know the area, but Tulalip is only about forty minutes north of Seattle. It is a native reservation, a good place to buy fresh salmon," Juan explains.

Raymond pipes in. "I'm going into the Marine Biology program. We are building salmon farms, and I want to educate our people and create jobs."

"I'm impressed. You have a goal that is good for the planet and good for your community. I wish I could come up with a plan like that. People in Mississippi need jobs too."

Raymond frowns. "I know something about catfish, but I have a hunch the water in Mississippi is too warm for salmon."

Juan says, "The salmon used to go all the way to Yakima, but since the dams were built, they can't travel as far."

I want to know what Juan plans to study.

"I plan to become a teacher. A lot of children travel with their parents who are migrant workers. They move around between schools as the harvest changes. Many don't speak English, and many of us feel we could help them learn, especially if more Spanish-speaking people worked in the schools."

I think about how each of them has a different focus for his studies but how each one wants to help his community.

"I said that I want to study history, but the real thing I care about is making the justice system fair for all of us. I like history because how can we move forward unless we understand the past? Part of change is getting people to vote. We can't make changes if we can't vote."

Waiters serve our meals, and we hear the call to order. I am bursting with more questions to ask but realize I'll see these guys again and so listen to the program.

I recognize the professors from the orientation who sit on a dais and take turns speaking. Each shares personal stories and encouraging messages for the new students.

By the time the servers remove the dessert plates, I'm remembering I am still a country boy who has rose with the rooster. Because of this, I turn into a wallflower when the party starts. I don't mind, though, because there is plenty to watch. Sets from different states dance to some new and old soul tunes. Then a reenactment of *Soul Train* begins.

Lamar emerges again as a leader and playfully introduces the LA dance moves out loud. Creed and Janice introduce the Seattle cohort of five dancers to new party tunes. Toni and Harold, visiting from WSU, dance to "Party Over Here Party Over There."

It goes on and on. Finally, the Tacoma Groove party turns the joint out roller skating to Harold Melvin and Gladys Knight.

I rock back and forth in my old shoes and sport coat. It's fun to see them all having fun, but it has been a long day, and I am tired. I place my hat on my head and say my goodbyes to the folks I met.

Then I call out to Lamar: "Hey, I'm leaving. See you next week."

He waves back and shouts, "Be cool, Ed," all without missing a beat of "Boogie Down Broadway." Exhausted from the long day, I slide through the closest door and head toward the elevator. *I'm still the guy who prefers reading books to sweating up my nice, crisp clothes.*

I ride the evening bus to Boren and Madison. It's eleven o'clock, late. When I finally enter Aunt Mary's apartment, I'm careful not to wake anyone. I pull out my journal before my head hits the pillow.

> *I feel like I'm living in a fairy tale, and I'm afraid I'll wake up and it will all go away. I went to the EOP orientation and welcome party today. There was so much excitement that the program was actually up and running in full swing. After a year of protest, the state passed a bill. The university and the government allocated money. They hired people, and the word went out. I never would have found out about it if Aunt Mary and Aunt Fran hadn't been paying attention for me. The mission of the program is to support students marginalized by poverty who want to succeed in careers that traditionally*

are reserved for people with money. But it's not just that they opened the door and let me in; they thought of what I'd need so that if I have trouble keeping up, I can get help. I'm feeling very lucky today.

I worry about myself a little, a country boy competing in classes with students from rich families where everyone went to college. They probably all talk like they do in books and travel to places I've only read about in an encyclopedia. That gets me worried. I just need to keep counting my blessings and try not to think about any of that comparison stuff.

I can find tutoring, mentoring, and social activities at the Ethnic Culture Center on Brooklyn Avenue. I kept a 2.30 grade point average in Mississippi while working full time at the KFC, without trying. Now, I'm living with Aunt Mary, closer to school and rent free, so I don't have to work and can put all my energy into school. I have a place to get help, and the professors have office hours, so I can go talk to them and get help. I should be able to at least keep up my grades at least as well as I did back home.

I'm going to write down the words my counselor said to me.

"You can do this. We looked at your transcript and reviewed your entrance essay and felt that you have the chops to do well."

I went through each course outline and found hope. My counselor, Gertrude, also explained how by accessing all the supports, I could crack the puzzle of university life. Coming to Seattle was an act of faith and so is becoming a student at U of W, and if I could escape Mississippi, I can work hard and get a college degree here.

32

DR. WATKINS

The next day, I travel back to the university to get my books and meet more professors. First, I go to the office of Dr. Charles Watkins, the professor for my Chaucer class.

A sign on his door reads, "All are welcome to the world of Chaucer." I really need to know who Chaucer is and why studying him will have anything to do with a nineteen-year-old from Vicksburg, Mississippi.

Dr. Watkins is a no-nonsense gentleman. "Welcome to my office, young man. You are an eager beaver, coming by before classes start."

I tell him my name is Wilson. Dr. Watkins is very polite and tells me all about the class.

"We will focus on the life and times of Chaucer. He was an English poet, author, and civil servant who became famous for writing the *Canterbury Tales*," explains Dr Watkins.

I'm going to need to spend time in the library just to figure out what Dr. Watkins is talking about.

Instead of showing my shortcomings, I thank Dr. Watkins for his time and head to the bookstore.

It is about a six-block walk and gives me a chance to calm my nerves before meeting my next teacher.

After standing in a long line, waiting to pay for my books, I'm at the check-out stand. The clerk sees the Chaucer book and says, "Dr. Watkins is a brilliant teacher. You'll really like his class. He is a fair grader too. He has high expectations, but if you don't cut class, you take good notes, and you keep up with the work, you'll do fine. That's $200.00 dollars for the books."

I find the $200.00 in my pocket and pay the kind clerk. *I'm glad I worked all summer and saved my money! College is going to be expensive.* I have yet to buy my blue books for exams, or any pencils and pens and all of the rest of the stuff I'll need. *I better pull some money from my savings.*

Despite the financial strain before even starting classes, it's turning into a beautiful September day, and I walk back to campus, using the map I got at the bookstore to find my classes. I'm pretty sure I could start school feeling much calmer if I know I won't get lost.

I have my books and everything I need to start my classes. I found my classes and know how long it takes to get to each one. I'm ready.

33

COMMUNITY SERVICE

BLACK STUDENT UNION

The Black Student Union and the Black Panthers see an opportunity to recruit support from the two hundred new students who've just joined the university through the EOP program.

I hear, "Come one; come all!" repeat all over campus during my first week at UW. I learn from Lamar how the Black Panthers partner with the Black Student Union to provide free breakfast for students in the Central Districts. I like that cause—it sounds like a good one to me—and want to support it.

There were many times I'd gone to school hungry when I was in Redwood, and I'm only here because of the work of groups like the Panthers and the Black Student Union.

So, during the second week of classes, I respond to the call. I go with Lamar to a meeting. The first man I meet is named Willie Brown. Willie explains that they raise money for the cause by selling papers on the Avenue. I really want to help, but I didn't want to commit to anything that would interfere with my studies.

"I could give you a couple of hours this Saturday, and then after midterms, if I'm doing OK, I could commit to once a week."

Willie says, "Hey man, you sell twenty-five to fifty papers in two hours, once a week, and you'll be setting up a hundred breakfasts a week for kids in the neighborhood."

That sounds great, so I agree to start that Saturday.

I know I just can't promise anything steady until after midterms. If I fail any of my classes, I'm going to be in big trouble. My family has gone out of their way to help me, and I don't want to disappoint them.

Willie is cool about all that and says, "Of course, whatever you can do can only help."

———

On Saturday, I walk all up and down the Avenue. There is a lot of traffic because of the football game versus Stanford, but not many people want to stop and buy a paper from me. But in spite of that, I think I'm making progress with pedestrians and shoppers. In an hour, I'm down to eight papers. When a man in a Ford pickup truck pulls up beside me and beckons, I mosey over. As I approach, I'm thinking I'm going to sell a paper, but I can't be more wrong.

The man in the truck shouts, "Why don't you [that bad word again] go back to Africa if you don't love America?"

My heart and mind travel from Seattle back to Mississippi in about two seconds. It feels as if I've just been spit on at St. Mary's after the game, though that was almost a year ago. Shocked and shaking, I step back and lean against a building to breathe and try to compose myself. And I realize I'm missing Melvin and James more than I ever thought possible.

Why is this happening to me? I am a do-gooder, taking classes, selling papers to help children, and not bothering anyone. I've worked for Boeing and KFC, live with family, and go to church. What do I have to prove to a jerk driving a big truck?

I kept on breathing and thinking about those children eating break-fast, starting the school day with full tummies, and that helps me get back to work. I keep at it until I sell all the papers, then walk back to the corner where Willie is working and give him the money. We shake hands and hit the other five on the other side, showing brotherly love.

I'm not planning on telling anyone about what happened on the cor-ner. I just whisper to myself, "Let it go today."

Today I learned I can travel between Seattle and Vicksburg in one second. I thought that the color of my skin didn't matter here, but I guess hate can live anywhere. I felt heat rise inside just like it did that evening I got spit on, but I calmed down and talked myself out of the anger.

Midterms are coming up, and I'm working hard to make sure I pass all my classes. I have a paper due for Chaucer that has me nervous, but I've set aside time to work on it. Now, every day it's getting dark a little earlier, and every day, the weather changes at least three times. I have to be careful not to leave my coat anywhere because it goes from cold to hot and wet to dry. I need to keep my focus and my eye on the prize and ignore those memories that want to block my success.

34

THE PILGRIM WAY

The first paper for Dr. Watkins is due on the third Monday of October. I find my favorite study carrel open at the library and methodically set out my notebook, pens, and pencils beside the Chaucer book. For five minutes, I stare at the blank page. Then I write my name and the name of the class. Still unable to think of what to write, I stare at the page for five minutes more. The second hand keeps moving, but the minute hand seems stationary on the clock up on the wall. Time is standing still.

My calendar confirms the necessity of this mission. This is the time to write the Chaucer paper. Tomorrow, I need to study for my oceanography exam and finish a paper for Dr. Llorens. This is the time I blocked out to be on track with Dr. Watkins. I read my notes and the directions for the paper again. Still nothing. *What does a story in a near-foreign language have to do with me? Why do I need to waste time on this?*

Realizing that is just talking myself down, I change my internal mindset. *You can't succeed at university if you question why you have to study something. You're just a country bumpkin. It's a good thing the university doesn't depend on you to come up with a curriculum.*

Then I remember the advice from orientation: "Ask for help. Use the resources."

That's it. I pack up my materials and walk over to Dr. Watkin's office.

"Wilson, how can I help you?"

I smile real big, happy that I'm receiving such a warm greeting.

"Dr. Watkins, sir, I'm here because I need help figuring out a thesis for my paper."

"Come on in and sit down. You're from Mississippi, right? Things are pretty rough down there, I imagine. I don't know if you know this, son, but I grew up in one of the poorest places in West Virginia.

"I still remember the day I first read, or should I say *tried to read*, the *Canterbury Tales*. I trampled over the language and was ready to throw the book right out the window. Luckily, my professor was a kindly man who understood. We talked about how different one story is from the other, just like on any journey when many people are traveling together. I imagine you ran into some of that on your trip up here from Mississippi. Is that right, son?"

"Yes, sir. I met all kinds of people, and sometimes, it seemed like the only thing we had in common was we were riding on a big, old Greyhound bus together. But the people in the stories were walking."

Dr. Watkins laughs. "Don't let the details get in the way. Think beyond.

"Where I grew up in coal country, every day, I watched the miners walk in a group to the mine. They all carried a lunch box and wore clean clothes and those helmets with lights. Then, at the end of their shift, they all came up out of the mine covered in soot, slumped over, and headed home together, a band of brothers who worked underground during daylight and staggered home in the dark."

I think of those men Dr. Watkins just described and of the way people in Redwood walk to the cotton fields and then wearily head home with calloused hands and bent backs—a community of workers following the same path, just like the coal miners.

"People make pilgrimages all the time. Did you look up the definition of *pilgrim*?"

"Yes, sir, a pilgrim is a person who goes to a religious shrine."

Dr. Watkins nods. "That's true. But that is a narrow definition for an old word. Always read a definition all the way through. We learn more about how a word carries meaning when we read the entire entry and then take time to understand the context of the word in the sentence. A pilgrim is also a wayfarer, a person who goes on a trip. It can mean to visit a religious site, but it can also mean to visit a place of some special meaning. It can also just be someone who takes a trip for a special reason. That's how I thought of the coal miners—every day taking a trip into the bowels of the earth looking for ore. How do you think the word pilgrimage applies to you?"

An idea is sparking in the back of my mind. "Well, sir, I left Mississippi to get an education and start a new life with my Seattle family who moved up here before World War II."

"Tell me about why your family moved up here."

"They were moving away from Jim Crow, looking for opportunities . . . could you call that a kind of pilgrimage? They found a FAME church, got good jobs, and bought homes."

"Young man, you sound like you are exploring a solid theme. Don't forget, Chaucer gave us the quote, 'Nothing ventured, nothing gained.' Think about how that ties in with the journeys you and your folks took. I think if you start writing about what the *Canterbury Tales* tells common people about taking risks and being a pilgrim, you will wind up writing a very interesting paper."

That little spark in the back of my mind is taking shape, and I feel like I just might have something to say about being a pilgrim. I thank the good professor for his time and return to the library where I get right to work.

Right now, I feel pretty good. I was wondering how I'd ever come up with something to say about Chaucer. I guess I didn't want to write the paper and started making up excuses. Then I remembered, ". . . our doors are open; we want you to succeed," and I asked for help. Not only did I get help, but now I'm excited to really read Chaucer and figure out for myself why he is required for most students who wind up pursuing a college education. I was thinking it was some ancient plan that had nothing to do with modern living, but maybe I was wrong. I'm just feeling good because I can get that paper written in two hours, and now I can stay on schedule for working on my other classes.

35

THE EASY PAPER

The next day, I talk to Professor Llorens before I set up shop in the study carrel. I think I have a good idea for a paper. The class is about Civil Rights, and I am from a place where people know all about the struggle to live without rights and the struggle to get them. This time, my dilemma isn't that I don't know what to write, but that I'm worried about having too much to say.

Professor Llorens welcomes me in and listens carefully. First, I thank him for his time, tell him I enjoy the class, and also let him know I am glad to have such a usable course outline.

I also share that for one of my papers, I'd like to tell about the Civil Rights struggle in Vicksburg. I see five different issues that need to be addressed, and I don't want to leave any of them out because they are all equally important.

"Professor Llorens, in Mississippi, Black people still live in poverty. Poor children can't always stay in school. People are stuck with poor housing, where their leaky roofs don't give protection from the rain and homes get swept away when it floods. They can't vote to change anything, even though they pay taxes because the system denies them their rights at the ballot box. Police brutality is a fact of life. And then, there is the problem with getting healthcare for families. Black folk in Mississippi get sick and can't get to the doctor because there ain't enough health centers in rural areas."

Professor Llorens nods. "You are forming a thesis for the argument that poverty is political. You've been thinking about this and have constructed a logical argument. I say, go with it."

I leave the office encouraged, and feeling like I could write a draft of this paper before I even catch the bus back to Aunt Mary's.

Today, I went to see Professor Llorens. I followed the adage from yesterday, "nothing ventured, nothing gained," and it paid off once more. Partly, I find it helpful to share my thoughts and ideas with someone who is intellectual. I never had that opportunity before starting here at the university. Maybe Miss Watson was the closest I came to having a teacher who encouraged discussion about ideas. I came away from my meetings with these two professors with the energy to learn and write. My mind gets focused and also reaches out, wondering and asking questions. This is more than I hoped for when I started out on this journey. At first, I just thought of getting a degree to get a good job, but now, I'm understanding that learning and discussing ideas is a reward in itself.

36

TRIP TO HALL HEALTH CENTER

By the sixth week of the first quarter, I have a good idea where I stand with my classes. I've completed all my papers that were due in English and Chaucer and have a *C-* average in Oceanography. The multiple-choice tests are hard, and it's a struggle to keep all the terms straight. I'm definitely feeling the stress of skating on the edge, the pressure like when you need to make that basket in the last five seconds of the fourth quarter. But I'm not ready to give up. I know that if he can just study harder, I'll make it.

The Wednesday before my Oceanography final, I talk to the professor. Dr. Veganman tells me that if I pass the final with a 75 percent, I will pass the class. That starts me thinking about how I can swing a 75 percent. The tutoring center offers me help. After all, I figure the point of a tutoring center is to help students learn how to learn. Maybe they can help me make a plan and help me decide how to prioritize time.

I visit the tutoring center and get the usual advice about going through the test, answering the questions I know for sure, then going back and finishing the rest . . . and how to figure out which choice is wrong right off the bat. But I don't leave feeling any more confident. Instead, I'm disappointed, feeling more worried than before I went there. On the bus ride home, I start to hiccup.

Back at home, Aunt Mary tells me to drink a glass of water while holding my breath. When that doesn't work, she calls up Mama Sallie, who tells me to put a paper bag over my head for ten minutes. When that doesn't work, Aunt Mary calls Aunt Fran, who tells me to swallow a tablespoon of vinegar. I'm still not any better.

By the time I finally fall asleep, I've tried ten different remedies, a different one from each church lady who Aunt Mary called. It's no surprise to me when I don't get any rest that night.

The next day, still suffering, I make my way to the Hall Health Center on campus for a medical solution.

There, Dr. Ballenger says, "Slow down, son. Exercise at the IMA, drink plenty of water daily, and quit eating so fast. You are in too much of a hurry, running for the bus, running for a class, running to the library. Do you ever slow down? You are going to run yourself crazy, Wilson. You are blowing all of your worries out of proportion."

Dr. Ballenger is a nice man who knows full well that I am struggling and worrying nonstop. *I don't think I'm going too fast; I'm just worried that I'm not going fast enough!*

I don't know if any of the cures is the reason, but the hiccups stop. If I ever get them again, I'm not complaining to anybody.

The hiccups finally stopped. I'm glad that I met Dr. Ballenger. I don't know whether he cured them or they just stopped, but I hope I never go through that again.

He gave me good advice about slowing down. I realized that I've been rushing because I ignore my successes and focus on my problems. I'll make a list of things I can feel good about:

- *I wrote a solid B+ paper in my Chaucer class for Charles Watkins. Dr. Watkins had me read my paper in class.*
- *I wrote a B paper in my Civil Rights class. Professor Llorens had me talk about Civil Rights in Vicksburg and*

Jackson, Mississippi, focusing on access to the ballot and overturning the "Grandfather Clause."

- Also, my Oceanography teacher told me that if I scored a C or better on the final, I would pass his class.

37

DREAMS

I am one jumbled mess the last weeks of the fall quarter as I try to sleep, study, and do well in my classes. Dreams of Redwood after the death of my mother haunt me. I often wake up still feeling the urgency in my sister's eyes. Bad dreams haven't bothered me since I got to Seattle, not until now. Lately, they've been crowding my sleep.

In many of the dreams, I'm sitting at the kitchen table, being confronted by my sisters. Daddy is there, too, but even though he is sitting with them at the table, he's absent. Dorothy and Bernice stare at him, unblinking. They don't talk, but I feel their suffering. Daddy stares at his mug of coffee, his head and shoulders drooped around him like armor. Nothing I say or do stops the pain. Even though I know it's pointless, I look to Daddy for help. I want to defend against their silent rebuke. *What choice did I ever have?* I want to run but am stuck, paralyzed, unable to speak. They are waiting. For what? They won't say. They keep staring and waiting, and I feel powerless.

I wake up confused and tired. *What am I supposed to understand from these dreams? What are they waiting for? Why does Daddy look so defeated? Why do I feel like they blame me? Daddy was the one who hurt everybody. Why do I feel like they expect something from me?*

My rational side takes over. *Dad should apologize to me, not the other way around.* I do my best to sweep the dream away. It is finals week—not the time to analyze dreams or indulge in self-analysis. I get dressed and go for a run.

While I run, I repeat formulas that are sure to be on the Oceanography final. Back home again, I take a shower and get dressed for school.

But still the dreams continue. The next night, spirits say, "Forgive him. We don't know how many days we have on earth. Help your sisters, your father, and yourself so you all can move past anger."

I wake up with the thought, *It's not about him; it's about me. But he's the one who beat me and was cruel to my mother. It's true. I badmouthed him and wasn't respectful, but I had a good reason. He should be the one to apologize, not me.*

That day, even after diligently working to stay focused, I feel like ants are crawling up my arms and my brain is in a fog. Lately, I feel like I'm carrying the burden of unfinished business a lot. But then, I am a college student; don't students always feel the pressure to be finishing something? There must be a message.

Both Mama Sallie and Mama Lanky believe in the power of dreams and tell me, "You need to pay attention to them." I think dreams become realities in daily life unless we pay attention to the warnings.

Again the next night, I sit at the kitchen table with my father and sisters. Daddy is hunched over a mug of coffee in defeat while my sisters look to me expectantly, as if I can do something to help. The promise I've broken to Mama haunts me, and I have to do something.

> *I'm barely keeping up with my classes. I'm worried about Dorothy and Bernice. Daddy is calling to me through my dreams. The only thing I can think to do is to see them. It's a long trip and my Seattle family may not understand, but if I don't go, I'm afraid I won't be able to keep up with my studies. I've worked hard to let go of the anger and forgive Daddy. Maybe I need to take the next step and talk to him and the girls.*

38

SEEKING HELP

"Dr. Veganman, is it possible to take the final exam early?" My reason is simple. "Sir, I have an early flight on the thirteenth of December, the same morning as our final. I would appreciate it, sir, if you allowed me some time and space to take the exam sooner."

Dr. Veganman's response is swift and straight-forward. "No."

I'm startled at his response to a seemingly simple request. The professor goes on in his thick accent, "Look, son, what would other students think if I allowed you to take the exam early? Plus, you might just blab your mouth and tell the other students the questions after taking the exam."

Honestly, I'm tired of the old curmudgeon. "I am not a blabber, and I don't have any contact with other students in the class of over 250 students. I haven't spoken to anyone, and no one has spoken to me," I calmly explain to Dr. Veganman.

The professor doesn't change his mind. I have to solve the problem without taking the test early. Even though my face is hot with frustration, I thank my professor and leave the office.

Later that day, I run into Lamar at the HUB. "I need your help, man. Can you give me a ride to the airport? I'll be able to take the final and catch my flight if I can get a ride. The final is early, and I can meet you in front of the HUB. Does that work for you?"

169

Lamar says, "No problem."

The ocean class at the UW Fall 1969 took no prisoners. The class was hard, and I found maintaining a C- in the class difficult. However, I did not drop the class. I'm not a quitter and wanted to stick with it until the end.

39

MY TRIP BACK

Lamar is good to his word, and meets me at the HUB. We stop by Aunt Mary's so I can pick up my suitcase and a bag of gifts. Then we drive into the Central District so I can say goodbye to Aunt Francis.

Over the last several weeks, the conversation with my family about spending Christmas in Mississippi has been difficult. When I added the part about stopping in Detroit, Aunt Francis reacted as if I'd lost my mind.

"Who in their right mind would go to Detroit in December? Boy, do you have any idea how cold it is? I know your daddy has been trying to keep his job and stay sober, but don't let that distract you from your future. You can visit your sisters in the summer, or during Spring Break. Why now?"

I tried to explain, but her exasperation didn't quit.

I hope she'll be more understanding now that Christmas is getting closer, and I hope that having Lamar along will make the meeting less personal.

The visit is brief. Aunt Francis is polite to Lamar and insists on a big hug from me. She even gives me gifts to take to Daddy and my sisters. "You do what you need to do, but we expect you back fresh and ready for the first day of your winter quarter." I understand.

Lamar gets me to the airport on time, and I board a Boeing 727 from Seattle to Detroit on December 18, 1969. That date is important 'cause it's my first time on a plane. I had worked at Boeing and dreamed of this day. Now it is here. Instead of grasshoppers in my belly, I have a chorus in my heart.

The flight is uneventful, and I have time to think about how I'm going to organize a meeting with Daddy and my sisters.

Bernice keeps her promise and pulls up at the arrival zone at the airport right on time. She is driving Mrs. Black's Lincoln Town car. We have a wild hug and laugh together on the sidewalk.

Bernice said, "I'm so glad to see you. I've missed you!"

I have barely seen my sisters, not really much at all after I moved into the Vicksburg YMCA.

"Bernice, look at you! You can't be that same skinny girl who couldn't reach the gas pedal. You're all grown up. I can't believe how much you've changed!" I can't stop staring at the young woman—tall, poised, and wearing high heels. But we have to get moving, so I don't linger. I slip into the car and let her take charge.

We start by talking about the usual things. She asks about the flight, the weather, and the family. I want to have a more serious conversation before we meet up with Daddy. When the conversation gets a lull, I ask, "Bernice, can we stop somewhere where we can talk about a few things before we get together with Daddy?"

"Of course. I've got just the place where we can talk quietly. There's a cafe a few miles from the house."

Late afternoon turns out to be a good time to find a quiet table. We choose a comfortable booth tucked away in the corner, a good setting for a serious conversation.

But I skirt the subject before digging into the history that was sure to make Bernice uncomfortable. "How is Dad doing after the bus ride from Lima?"

"He complained about some back and knee pain, but he rested well. Otherwise, he is being his old self. Dad likes to talk about Pat Scott and

Uncle James in old Mississippi and deer hunting with a high-powered rifle."

"I'll bet the deer won't miss him."

Bernice laughs. "They knew to be scarce when they heard Daddy thumping through those woods. You wouldn't have needed to bring all that chicken if he had been a better hunter. June, you must have more than that on your mind than bus rides and deer. What's going on? You must have something big on your mind to want to go to a restaurant to talk."

"I want to have an honest group conversation over dinner with Dad about some stuff we swept under the rug for years. Bernice, we need to talk about what happened when we were kids and ask Dad for forgiveness for us bad-mouthing him behind his back. We also need to state up-front how we feel about him merging two families after our mother died in 1964. I'm the oldest child of our original family, and I want to apologize to him and see if we can get him to say how he feels about pushing Mrs. Mae and her kids on us as we were still grieving. What do you think?" I pause for a minute, then surge on. "What do you think about me raising these questions and issues with him? I feel bad that I didn't fulfill my promise to Mama about taking care of you and Dorothy. It had to be bad for the both of you. All I know is that the promise I made, set next to all that we faced, is making it hard for me to move on. I need to make an opportunity to mend the bridges and learn how to make peace with the past."

All the time I'm speaking, I watch Bernice's face for clues. She doesn't nod or smile. Her eyes narrow, staying focused on me, and her face is still. She keeps her hands still, too, the right one resting on her water glass and her left hand set palm down beside her fork.

Finally, she speaks slowly, in a steady, controlled voice. "It's best to let sleeping dogs lay in the same spot. Why unearth this stuff right before the Christmas holidays?" She said, "I am all over the past and 1964. It's 1969 in Michigan."

I nod but counter. "I feel 1964 pushing into 1969. I am who I am because of the past. Right now, I'm doing my best to go beyond that, but I know I won't find the person I need to become if I don't go back to

1964 and make repairs. What about you, Bernice? You're going to graduate from high school soon; you've got a good situation working for Miss
B. I can't believe she lets you drive her car. What about after high school?
Have you thought about going to college? Opportunities are opening up
every day. Do you think you can grab them when you still can't look back
without getting punched in the stomach? Maybe so far, you've been able
to move ahead without making peace with all the difficulties you faced.
You never know when those old feelings are going to rise up and smack
you backwards. Does it hurt knowing Daddy chose Miss Mae's children
over us? It might help to get an apology."

We sit in silence for a few minutes before Bernice speaks again. Her
face softens, and her eyes brighten with tears, but she holds them back.
"June," she says, "I've been making my own way as long as you have. I
get through each day by focusing on right now, not by raking up terrible
memories. Brother, I love you, I can hear you, and I'll support you. You're
determined to go ahead with this meeting, and I will be there right along-
side you, but I'm only agreeing to this because I love you."

"Bernice, we have to get this stuff out front," I beg her.

It is dark when we pull up to the house. Bernice and Dorothy start
fixing dinner while I go upstairs to visit with Mama's elderly cousin, Alma
Black. Alma has been married to a man from Mississippi who found work
in Detroit in the early '50s. They're making a good living working for the
Ford auto manufacturer. They bought a three-bedroom home and can
afford nice cars. Now Mrs. Black is bedridden but still sharp. I'm happy to
see that my sisters take good care of her.

"June, come here and give me a kiss! The girls are so excited that their
college brother came to visit. We are all so proud of you. I only wish your
Mama was here to see how handsome you are."

I grab her hand. "I hope my sisters are taking good care of you; if they
aren't, you let me know."

"They don't give me any cause to complain. So you all are here for a
family reunion. How are you feeling?"

I don't want to say too much. "A lot of water has washed under that old bridge. I'm just hoping to keep our family ties strong, especially since we're all spread out away from Mississippi.

Mrs. Black nods. "You got that right, June. Family needs to stay together, even when they get tossed apart."

I know my sisters have a good relationship with Mrs. Black. They get to live in her home, drive her car, and have a grocery allowance. They keep the house and yard clean and make sure that the elderly lady is clean and well fed. I think that Mrs. Black makes a good point about the importance of family. Me and my sisters had been through some tough times, but it is the extended family that stepped in and lifted them out of the worst of it. Because of caring grandparents, aunts, uncles and cousins, they can survive and find opportunities.

I hear a muffled cough and a rustle, turn, and see my father standing in the doorway.

"Wilson senior, stop lurking around there and come in and say hello," says Mrs. Black.

He walks in and holds his hand out for me to shake.

I take it and pull Daddy in for a hug. In that embrace, I feel Daddy exhale and grip me a little tighter before he lets go. "It's good to see you, son. Fran and Margaret are really proud of how well you're doing out there. So am I."

I feel tears fill my eyes. I hide my face and say, "Thanks, Dad. It's been a long trip. I'm going to take a shower before dinner."

When I get out of the shower, I smell home cooking throughout the house. My stomach growls, and I go to find out when we're eating.

Bernice and Dorothy have just pulled a glazed ham out of the oven. One of his sisters had scored it with diamonds and decorated it with cherries and pineapple. Whole green beans lay in a china dish under a blanket of melting butter. Molded fruit salad topped with whipped cream wobbles on the table. Set aside on the counter, I spy a sweet potato pie and breathe in the warm scent of cinnamon.

Dorothy sees my reaction and says, "Just in time. You can slice the ham."

Then she and Bernice add plates of hot biscuits and scalloped potatoes to the counter.

I've never seen so much food on this family's table and wonder where my sisters learned how to cook. I'm grateful to Mrs. Black for how well my sisters live in her house.

"June, go find Daddy. Let's not let all this good food get cold," Bernice says.

There is no need to find Daddy. He is walking toward the table. "I got it, Bernice. My eyesight might not be what it was, but I still have a good enough nose to lead me to a fine meal."

It is fine. Junebug cherishes every bite, trying to force himself not to eat too quickly. Everything tastes great, especially the pie. We don't talk much during the meal, and I help to clear the table. By the time dessert is over and the table is clear, I figure I better get the meeting started.

"Daddy, there are some things we need to talk about, and I want Dorothy and Bernice to stay, listen, and tell their stories. It wasn't right about the way I left the house and left Mississippi, and I want to apologize for my unkind behavior toward you. I bad-mouthed you to Grandma Lankie and my sisters because I was angry, but I know it was wrong. Even though I love you, and I know I made a promise to help my sisters, I left to live at the YMCA because I couldn't find it in my heart to accept Miss Mae or her children. I knew they were my blood through you, but I couldn't find the love to stay."

I pause, catch my breath, and look at Daddy, and, for a moment, feel like I am living inside my dream. Daddy is bent over his coffee mug, and his sisters are staring at him.

I push forward. "Now, I want to forgive you for leaving us adrift after Mama's death. She was your wife who birthed five children while she was alive. I forgive you for attempting to merge two families into one. Whatever you had in mind, it did not work. You caused a lot of pain in 1964; we were like ships sailing in the dark. We might have been the same color,

Dad, but we didn't live with the same values. I will not blame Miss Mae. You caused emotional damage to both families. Mama said on her death-bed that she wanted me to be the man of the house because she couldn't trust you, and she knew you didn't have the gumption to take care of her children first. She ended up correct. I did not have the wherewithal to cook, bring in a check, or wash the dishes. You brought us into this world with a sick mama, and when she died, you abandoned us, leaving us rud-derless. The man who was supposed to provide for us brought three more children under our roof and left us to fend for ourselves."

I point my finger at Daddy and ask, "What do you have to say to the leftovers of your damaged family today, December 23, 1969?" It sounds harsh, I know, but I also know if I don't get it all off my chest, my future will be handcuffed to my past, dragging me down to the depths of noth-ing good.

Dad, Wilson Sr., had listened in silence, his forearms holding the weight of his shoulders, his chest hunched around his mug, and his chin hung over his chest. Finally, he speaks in a hushed voice.

"I was in a boatload of pain from the war. What I did was selfish and wrong to both families. After the war, all I cared about was finding dis-tractions: getting drunk; playing cards; avoiding work and responsibility. I loved all of my children and their mothers, but I didn't show it the way a man should—by being faithful and providing support."

He pauses and looks up, searching each of our faces. "Please forgive me for my selfish behavior. I know I was wrong and don't blame you for your anger. After the war, I never found my bearings, and I tried to run away from the pain. I hurt everyone and never found my way or my gifts. Excuses won't change the wrongs. What I did to my family was wrong and caused harm to all of you, and I'm ashamed. The horror of war, what I saw and what I took part in defending the flag, was more than I could bear. Liquor seemed like it drowned out the pain, but it made it worse when I had to face the pain I caused my family.

"My ammo truck in the colored unit blew up, and we had to walk sixty miles through the jungle with our rifles and gear. We walked through the swamps of the jungle, all the time fearing enemy fire or capture. Soaked to the bone, we tramped through the snake-infested water, not knowing when we'd find our troops. I can never tell what I saw, or the suffering I witnessed during that war. They gave us cigarettes for courage, along with booze, smokes, and pain pills. All that helped after we found our company, but nothing helped the nightmares that started when I got home. I wish I could have strung together my skills as a farmer, plumber, or bricklayer and become a productive man of note, but every time I tried, I fell and waited for someone who cared about me to pick me back up. Willie B., my loving wife took the brunt of my anger and pain. I beat you, Junebug, in a fit of rage with a razor belt more than once, when I was drunk. The booze was talking when I beat you with my belt, welts grew on your body, and I didn't stop. I beat you out of rage."

He stops. His eyes are wet and his hands trembling. He looks directly at us, each in turn.

"We did not have VA counseling for colored soldiers down in Vicksburg. Maybe I was too embarrassed to seek help from the folks over in Jackson. I was ashamed, thinking people would find out and laugh at me and the Reed family. Junebug, my Mama Sallie covered over and over for my behavior. She covered for my drinking, and she covered for my arrests over on Highway 61 at the Juke Joint on Friday nights. Mama covered for my wasting money that was meant for food. You once saw me come home in the back seat of the police car. It was my fault you five went hungry and depended on welfare commodities. All of you suffered because I was a half of a man, trying to do right but ended up doing wrong. Mama Sallie felt sorry for me and never wanted our dirty laundry out in the public. What can I do to mend and repair the hurt and pain I caused?"

As the oldest, I speak up and say, "You can formally apologize to each of us in private in the next day or so."

During the whole speech, I gave Daddy my full attention, only glancing occasionally at my sisters. Now, I see the youngest, Dorothy, is upset. Tears stream down her face.

"Daddy, I just want to say that I am not in a forgiving mood right now. What good is an apology going to do me now? When Mama died, I was eight years old. I was just a little girl, and who cared about me? I lost my Mama who loved me and made sure I had something to eat, who made sure I had clean clothes, and who kissed my hurts away. You brought in your woman from down the road and her kids to crowd up our shack. You replaced our Mama with a woman who barely bothered to even help her own kids, let alone do anything to help us. I got left to fend for myself at eight years old. Lucky for me, Mama Lankie let me come over when I was hungry and found me clothes to wear. How is a child supposed to forgive a parent for the hurt you piled on? I can't sit here anymore, and I sure don't want to have any more to do with you."

She delivered most of her speech from her seat at the table, but as her courage grew, she stood to face them. Her anger is directed at all three of them, but she directs the brunt of her words to her blubbering father. Finished, she turns her back on them and rushes out of the room.

Bernice stands. "Dorothy's right. It's one thing to admit you were wrong and another to understand what you put us through. I don't want a private apology; the public one was bad enough. I'm going to check on my sister. You need to walk a little further through that swamp and acknowledge more about how your actions affected us. It wasn't just going hungry from time to time, or the embarrassment of knowing that I could find my drunk father at the bar. It was all the things we missed and things we had to figure out for ourselves without a mother or a father who cared. I'm going to check on Dorothy."

Me and Daddy sit alone at the table for a few minutes. He weeps. I seek to console. *Why did I think I could orchestrate a family meeting that would heal the wreckage of a decade?* I was wrong to think a meeting would take the pain away. Every wound is opened, and every scab is red from being picked. Both of my sisters are in tears, and my father is bent in defeat. *What should I do now?*

I get Daddy a glass of water. After a while, the old man sips it. He wipes his eyes and looks up at me.

"You are growing into a fine man, son. Thank you for what you did. I needed to hear all that, and I need to remember how my drinking hurt my children."

"Daddy, I'm sorry. Fighting you back in Vicksburg and bad-mouthing you to the family was wrong. It was easier thinking about my wants and needs and blaming you for going without. I blamed you for Mama's dying, and for the fear I felt not knowing how to take care of my sisters. How was I supposed to cook or take care of the house? After Mama died and Miss Mae came to live with us, I figured no one needed me, and I could leave. Today, I was wrong to think I could fix it all with a dinner meeting."

"Wilson, I quit drinking, and I accepted Jesus as my Savior. Every day, I turn my life over to Him. That's the only thing I can control—knowing that only the Lord controls anything. Give your sisters time. They've had to bottle up all those feelings for four years, and they have a lot to be angry about. I'm truly sorry for the pain that I caused, and I am proud of you. Thank you for all the help you gave your sisters and me. You stepped up, and you put your family first. Now you are setting an example, and maybe your sisters will see that they can make something of their lives. Mississippi is the home of the Blues, Wilson. We know about the Blues, and we know about family, love, and survival. Let your sisters have their Blues and let yourself feel them too. Then let yourself grow and become the man you have inside yourself."

We're both tired—I can sense it—and so we talk a little while about ordinary things like the weather and how proud we are of Bernice and Dorothy for speaking their minds and for taking such good care of Mrs. Black while going to school. Within an hour, we go to bed, sharing the extra bedroom. And we both sleep heavy. I don't even dream.

The next morning, I go in the kitchen and find Bernice scrambling up diced ham and eggs. Fresh coffee is perking on the stove, and there is a big pitcher of orange juice. Dorothy is at the table, guarded but willing to talk about general things. I am polite, not pushy, and take Daddy's advice to stay out of her way.

Bernice sets the last dish on the table, sits down, and says, "Let's hold hands and pray that the Lord looks down on us, forgives us our sins, and helps us to live in the Spirit of love and forgiveness forever after."

Each Reed offers their hands to the one beside them, each squeezing the hands they hold. We all bend our heads and together say, "Amen."

Dinner didn't go the way I planned. I thought I could manage it so that everyone said their peace, and then we'd all be grateful and full of Christian charity. Each of us said our peace, it just wasn't what I expected. I always thought Dorothy was too young to remember anything about Mama, and that since she was the youngest, I figured she got all the attention. I was wrong. Here, the youngest was the most vulnerable and neglected. Once again, I got shoved off of my assumptions. At least, Daddy and I said our peace to each other, and Dorothy and Bernice got to hear him admit he was wrong and apologize. I feel a certain peace now, and I can't remember when the last time was that I felt this calm. No more grasshoppers. At least, about this.

40

BACK IN THE SOUTH

My plan is to visit Vicksburg so I can see my family and close friends back home. Before leaving Seattle, I went shopping at Frederick and Nelson, the premier department store in Seattle. I imagined returning to Mississippi just like Santa Claus, carrying a sack of presents. I want to share some Christmas love with a few special folks. Before leaving Detroit, I stash a pile for the family under their tree as a surprise before I leave.

Mrs. Black suggests Daddy take the Lincoln to drive me to the airport. My sisters meet me at the porch to wish me well. Bernice whispers, "June, I love you. I know you are going to make something important of yourself. You're made of steel. You got out of Vicksburg, found a way forward when anyone else might have given up, and you took the bus, alone all the way to Seattle, where even your family were almost strangers. That took more courage than I can imagine."

Dorothy wraps her arms around my chest. "Keep in touch."

The departure drop off area is crowded, but me and Daddy manage time for a brief goodbye. Daddy gets out of the car and gives me a big hug. "I love you, and I'm proud of you, son. You are on the way to becoming a fine man."

I feel happy, hugging my father like that, and sincerely say, "I love you, Daddy. I'll call."

I stride up the ramp to the idle plane thinking I'll be able to have a good rest on the flight. Even when a lady rushes up, bumps into me, and pushes through the line as if she is the pilot heading for the cockpit, I am unphased.

Once buckled into my seat, it takes me several minutes to realize I am sitting next to the lady who elbowed her way past her fellow passengers in her hurry to get to the front of the line.

I wrestle with what to say—if anything. At last, I settle into my usual routine: reading and enjoying the view from my window seat.

The take-off is smooth. I'm looking forward to the three-hour flight as a chance to rest and read without trying to figure out what will be on final exams. It's a rare opportunity to let my mind stop working and just daydream.

But disappointment finds me on that plane. As soon as we are at altitude, the pilot makes an announcement. "We will hit some turbulence soon. Please keep your seatbelts on until further notice."

My seatmate doesn't take the news well. She stirs and mumbles to herself. Then we hear a loud *boom* and enter a massive storm. The plane drops, and the lady beside me screams, "Please Lord, do not let us die!" She grabs my arm, digs her fingernails into my skin, and buries her head into my shoulder, screaming over and over, "Help us, Lord. Help us!"

The plane keeps on bouncing and shaking through the turbulent storm. Finally, after about twenty minutes, it steadies. The pilot's calm voice reassures the passengers, and it seems like the emergency is over. Unfortunately, the woman beside him is still panic-stricken, crying and clutching my arm. I don't want to pry her fingers off me, so I wait. Eventually, the flight attendants came around with the beverage cart, and the woman asks for a cola.

She never speaks to me, let alone thanks me for allowing her to cling to me like a thorny vine. And I go to wondering whether she has something going on in her life that makes her extra edgy, extra prickly, or if she is always this nervous when she takes off in an airplane. I guess I'm just trying to be curious, not judgmental is all.

I don't really want to think about what would have happened if we crashed. Now that I'd finally made peace with Daddy and my sisters, I want to look ahead, knowing that even with everyone spread across the country, we're still kin.

Like the way you get shaken up while watching a horror movie and then feel calm and relieved when it's over, the passengers on Flight 125 are calm now that the plane is steady and the seatbelt signs are off. We are flying above the clouds—not much to see—and I am exhausted. I rest my head against the window and close my heavy lids.

I don't wake up until the plane has landed and my seatmate is pushing her way down the aisle, trying to be the first one off the plane. I don't imagine I'd soon forget this flight from Detroit—the flight where I was mauled by a fearful woman.

I arrive in Mississippi at noon. It's cold and crispy with no wind, a comfortable December day. My best friend ,who I've known since grade school, Arthur, and his wife, Marie, are waiting at the airport baggage claim to pick me up.

I'm feeling all excited to see them, so much so that I slip and fall on the floor running forward to greet them. I hug them both and say, "Thanks for coming to pick up an old country boy like me."

Arthur helps me with my stuff. I am carrying my small luggage and the load of presents. Arthur and Marie are wearing matching winter over-coats. Both say in unison, "Welcome home! It seems like years that you've been gone."

That's what marriage will get you. I keep my mouth shut for a minute before replying, "Thanks for picking me up."

We fill the forty-five-minute drive from the Jackson airport back to Vicksburg, catching up. Arthur asks questions about life at the university, and in Seattle. He wonders about my northern family and also asks about Daddy and my sisters in Detroit. He even finds time to talk about his two favorite subjects: hunting and fishing.

I tell the story about my flight. Arthur enjoys a good laugh, and I do too. I keep thinking how amazing it is that a little time and distance can change our perspectives and turn terror into humor.

When we got close to Vicksburg, Arthur asks, "Where are you staying?"

"At the Howard Johnson near the Civil War Battlefield."

When Arthur drops me off, I tell him I want to rest. But I also tell Arthur, in no uncertain terms, I'd pay him like a taxi driver and for gas to drive me around town.

"I want and need some Seattle money!" I give him fifty dollars as a down payment on the job of driver and then ask him to pick me up in the morning. We are from Redwood, way out in the country, where family is not just blood family. We come from a place where loyalty and love, not just who you are related to, is what cements family and relationships.

Alone in my room, my mind whirs. *You are back in your neck of the woods. Bigfoot country, where everything is what it seems. Folks keep life real slow and manageable.* I look forward to visiting some family, James and Melvin, and an old girlfriend named Trudy.

It's real nice having a whole motel room to myself. I eat the sandwiches and sweet potato pie that Bernice packed for me, take a long, steamy shower, and fall asleep watching the old Jimmy Stewart movie, *It's a Wonderful Life.*

Arthur honks outside my door at 9:00 a.m., sharp.

"Today, just take me to my Mama Lankie, please."

We'd done enough catching up earlier to ride for a while without talking. Christmas music plays on the radio. And I hum along with Otis Redding's "Merry Christmas, Baby" while watching the scenery. I look out on the homes and streets decorated with lights and Santa Clauses. My heart—the part you can feel—feels full with the happiness of being *home for Christmas.*

Arthur pipes up, "People down here in Mississippi love the good ole days." He speaks like a Yankee that moved back home, but it fits my mood, so I agree.

I like not having formal plans for the next few days. After all, I know a little something about what could happen when you fly in and out of Mississippi: You can have some real fun, and side by side, get yourself in a whole lot of trouble being single and unattached. I'm ready to let loose a little and have some of that fun.

The drive to Mama Lankie's takes us a ways back into the country, and I watch the brown-leafed trees pass. After living in the city for so many months, I am calmed by the drive out in the country near Vicksburg.

Mrs. Lucy and Mama Lankie live across the street from one another, so meeting them together is easy. Arthur drops me off and says he will roll back through in a couple of hours.

I want to keep the presents a surprise, so I slide the bag under the porch rocking chair and pound on Mama Lankie's door several times. Finally, she peeps through the side window curtains and screams, "Boy, stop beating on my door! I ain't hard of hearing."

My smile stretches from ear to ear. I'm happy to be back home. She bursts through the door and throws her skinny arms around me. "My college boy's come back home to see me!" she exclaims.

I get busy hugging and squeezing my dear grandmother, the tiny woman, all of five feet tall and maybe a hundred pounds when wet, while tears flow down my cheeks. She's happy as the dickens, too, and I say, "Mama, how have you been doing the last few months?"

Her response is quick. "Going to church and praying on my knees every morning, visiting the doc, and gossiping with Mrs. Lucy across the street. What else is there to do down in this hollow under the hill?"

"Nothing is wrong with gossiping among good friends as long as no one gets hurt."

"You got that right."

We go inside, and I sit down at her table.

"I'm going to call Mrs. Lucy and make us a nice pot of tea," she says.

I offer to help but find out quickly that is a mistake. She shushes me to stay in my seat.

Then she dials Mrs. Lucy's number with the receiver tucked under her chin as she busies herself in the bright little kitchen. The conversation is short. Mama Lankie tells me Mrs. Lucy wants to spruce up a little before she comes over but will be here shortly.

I sit and watch my grandmother fill the teakettle, light the burner, and set out her chipped teapot with the blue flowers and matching tea cups. It feels so good to watch her do these simple things; I want to hang on to the moment, so I ask about her flowers because that is a topic I know she'll enjoy talking about.

The water boils, and I want to jump up and pour the water into the teapot, but I know better than to interfere. She doesn't spill a drop and carries the tray with the cups, saucers, sugar, and tea to the table. Then she goes back and fixes a plate with sugar cookies decorated in bright colors. She pours out two steaming cups and pushes the sugar at me. I pinch a cookie from the plate and set it on my saucer.

Mama Lankie tells me about my mama and her brother at another Christmas a long time ago. I've already heard the story many times, the one about Uncle Jimmy stealing cookies, selling them to his friends, and Mama getting even by baking a batch where she used cod liver oil instead of butter. But I love hearing it again. I can tell how much she enjoys the telling.

Then she wants to know about the family in Seattle. I start by telling her how everyone is doing—until she interrupts with what really interests her.

"When are you going to get married and have some chillens?"

I can't help but burst out laughing, and I keep laughing so hard the tea sloshes onto the saucer. I sober up when I catch the expression on Mama Lankie's face. She isn't laughing. She asks, "What's funny?"

"I am not laughing at you, Mama. It's just I'm barely nineteen, and I'm way too busy to even date, let alone start a family."

"Plenty of young men your age get married and start families. You need a good woman to take care of you."

I try to make my point, knowing full well, deep inside, she ain't going to see it any other way. "Mama, I want to get married and have children someday, but I hope I learned enough from how I grew up to wait until I get my education and a steady job. Kiddies will have to wait. I'm still learning to take care of myself."

A loud knock at the door interrupts us. Mama Lankie complains, "Of all days, why is everybody knocking so loud?"

I jump up and let Mrs. Lucy in. She grabs me like it's old home week and shakes me and hugs me until I have to pull away to get my balance again.

We all spend awhile catching up. When the ladies start talking about soap operas, I go to the porch and bring in the presents. As I walk back inside with the big red bag, I say, "Ho, ho, ho! Santa's here."

With that, I whip out two presents, each wrapped in a special Frederick and Nelson forest green box with a red ribbon.

Mama Lankie exclaims, "Junebug, these are wonderful! I never expected any gifts from you. This is too much! You make sure and don't go spending all your hard-earned money on foolish things!"

I know she is scolding out of habit, and I'm happy to see her toes wriggling in the soft fabric of the new slippers.

Mrs. Lucy smiles and thanks me profusely. My heart melts to know they are delighted with their slippers.

"Thank you both for all the love you have shown this little country boy from Redwood, Mississippi. You've given me love and kindness all these years, and I just wanted to say thank you. I will cherish these memories and hold them in my heart always."

They laugh and cry. Tea time with Mama Lankie has always been special, but it's also sometimes been unnerving.

A moment later, I'm deciding how to answer her next question: "Are you going to see that girl who lives in the Bottom before you leave?"

"Yes, ma'am." Then I smile and whisper, "We are going to have to keep that topic on the down low. Trudy is a good friend with a good job a long way from Vicksburg, so there's nothing to talk about."

Gossiping is a way of life in small communities. I figure gossip is a way to make life more interesting, and bad-mouthing people might be a way to feel better about yourself. Then I think, *I do not miss the small-town gossip.*

Arthur's horn honks out front. "I have to get going now. Happy New Year, and I'll stay in touch." Grandma Lankie gives me another fierce hug. Mrs. Lucy promises to keep an eye on the little woman and kisses my cheek. I snatch up the last two cookies and wink. "I gotta share one of these with Arthur."

The women stand at the porch and wave goodbye as I settle into the car and Arthur sets the car in motion.

I am still feeling the admiration of the womenfolk as we roll down the street in Arthur's car, taking part in the daily, friendly ritual of waving hello, looking like rock stars, riding around town where everybody knows everybody.

I can't believe the spunk! I was worrying myself about leaving home, as if they needed me to take care of them. They are doing just fine without me. I just loved seeing their little feet in their new slippers. I hope I can come back again next year. Maybe next year, I should get them each a sweater. Riding around with Arthur is a hoot!

41

THE KFC

The next day, I put on my new navy-blue suit for a visit to my old job. I want to show my old work buddies that I've been making good on my goals and making good money after parting with the chicken shack.

Arthur picks me up and whistles. "I hope you aren't planning to cook chicken in that get-up," he laughs.

When we get there, Melvin shouts my name and rushes forward to give me a hug as he lets us in through the back door.

"Hey, man, you look like Al Green from Memphis," says Melvin when he gets a good look at my new duds.

We hit five like back in the day, and Melvin announces, "Junebug Wilson is here at the KFC shack for the Christmas holidays. OK, folks, give him a standing ovation."

Linda and Becky, the counter workers, barely look up, and the rest of the staff, all unknown to me, ignore us.

James looks at me like I've stolen a bucket of chicken. James offers no hugs or handshakes. Instead, he focuses on chicken sales and productivity, nodding, weaving and bobbing like a turkey.

I get the drift. Arthur and James have been close friends for a long time, and Arthur understands what's going on too. He goes over and hits

James five, looks at me, and says, "Hey, man, we got folks to see, and we have a date with ribs and macaroni and cheese."

"Take care, Melvin, and Happy Holidays, brother." I flash a peace sign to James.

As soon as we get back to the car, Arthur says, "Hey, man, James is mad that you left them high and dry when you went to Seattle. He didn't know what a good worker you were until after you left."

"Arthur, you remember what I was up against. I was thinking he would be happy for me."

"Truth be told," replies Arthur, "he has had five people in the six months since you've been gone. He is mad about having to hire and interview new people all the time to keep the kitchen stable. Mr. Robert Hanson, the owner, has been all over James about high turnovers."

"I'm done with the situation at KFC and probably shouldn't have rolled through the chicken shack." Though I don't understand how to think about the folks I left behind and am even more grateful for the solid opportunities I've found in Seattle.

I count my blessings and put the year behind me. I can forgive myself and everyone I slighted, never forgetting the year that was humbling, dangerous, joyful, and rewarding—all rolled into one big bowl of wax.

I wasn't thinking about how the guys from the KFC might feel about my flying into town, showing up in a new suit, and talking about college. Neither one of them went beyond the eighth grade. I was feeling so good about getting away from here, I thought they'd be happy for me, but I was wrong. James has had a tough go of it, but he's making good money and has his own opportunities. I'm pushing past Jim Crow, and so is James. Not long ago, he'd never be a store manager, and look at him now. I should have congratulated him on his success instead of showing up in a brand-new suit.

42

CONVERSATION WITH TRUDY

I want to reconnect with my high school girlfriend, Trudy. So I walk across town to visit her. Five days before Christmas, the weather is cool and clear. It is a familiar walk, and I use the time to decide what to say.

I almost didn't have the nerve to visit, but when I called, she insisted. Her voice on the telephone was so confident and cheerful that I relaxed.

"Wilson," she said, "Don't you even think of leaving town without visiting me! It's been too long. Plus, I want to hear all about life in Seattle and the University of Washington."

So this morning, here I am, heading out through the Mississippi morning mist, across town, to meet the girl that I still wish hadn't gotten away.

We didn't part well, and I blame myself and my desires for spoiling our friendship by trying to push her into more intimacy than we was ready for. Our friendship was based on the shared interests of doing well in school and learning about the world from books. I realize now how I'd pushed too hard and forced her to back away from me.

Today, I walk, hoping there is an opportunity to mend fences, and I hope we can, at the least, rekindle our friendship.

Folks in her neighborhood are sitting on their porches, visiting with passersby and enjoying the sunshine that has now burned through the mist. They greet me with a special recognition.

"Hey, got any chicken on you today?"

"Trudy's going to be glad to see you!"

I muse to myself, *Mississippi people have a great sense of humor*, and I'm happy, feeling at home. Then I let go of my ruminations to return their greetings.

"Good morning!"

"Happy New Year!"

"Beautiful day!"

Every ten feet it seems I'm responding to another well-wisher. By the time I get to Trudy's house, I've forgotten my apprehension. The grasshoppers have been silenced by the flood of kindness.

I don't even have to knock. She must have seen me walking toward her house because the door opens as soon as I approach.

"Wilson!" (She didn't like nicknames so never called me Junebug.) "Look at you, the college man from the University of Washington! You've put a little meat on your bones, and you're looking good."

"Trudy, you're a sight for sore eyes!"

She lets the screen door slam as she bursts through it to reach her arms up for a hug. It almost feels like old times, but the hug is brief, and Trudy pulls away without a kiss.

"Come on and sit down," she says. "I want to hear all about your trip and the university. Now that I have a good steady job, I'm planning to start at a university as soon as I have enough money saved."

I launch into a recap of my trip and good fortune.

Trudy stops me several times to ask questions and is especially curious about the EOP program. "With the tutoring help you're getting, you don't need my help anymore," she says with a wink.

I change the conversation to ask about her family.

"My folks are well here in town and in the Midwest. The snow and cold weather don't bother me as much as it does other folks."

She wants to know about my family and close friends. "Tell me about your dad and sisters and the good life in big Seattle."

"Trudy," I say, "I left Vicksburg just like you on a Greyhound headed for the Promised Land, looking for a job and a quality education with a family that was foreign. I only knew them from letters and phone calls."

I notice she is observing me while I talk. I'm not sure what she is thinking, so I go on. I want to paint a picture, plus it feels good to talk about the trip with her, a true friend.

"Trudy, I met some nice people on my 2,600-mile trip to Seattle. It made me think a lot about Mississippi and how small and tight our community is here. For a long time, I felt like I was venturing out into a big ocean from a small tad pool."

Trudy's mama brings us two glasses of lemonade and a plate of cookies. Her greeting is friendly but a little restrained. She says, "Wilson, it's been too long since we've seen you, but you sure look good. Did Trudy tell you about her job in Chicago? I'm so proud of how well she's doing. She'll take all she's learning at the real estate office and get herself a college degree in no time."

"Yes, ma'am." I reply. *I guess we're both moving on.*

After her mom goes back inside, I say, "It sounds like Chicago is agreeing with you."

"Yes, it is. I learned that I have the skills to get a good job and earn a good living in a real estate office. I'm a good administrator, and at work, I'm respected. Also, I now realize that even though we got a segregated education here in Vicksburg, we had each other's back and support systems. We had dedicated teachers helping us succeed and we could always get the help we needed. Like a lot of things, those who took getting a good education seriously, got one, segregated or not.

"One thing I like about the big city: there are lots of different ways to get to where you're going, and I'll find mine. Maybe EOP programs will come to Chicago, or maybe I'll be able to make it on my own."

I've always admired Trudy. She was the National Honors student and helped me maintain my *B-* average. I truly loved her in high school. She is smart, has a great sense of humor, and saw me as a cool dude to be around.

I had felt she loved and respected me and maybe also found me to be a good friend and companion.

I've missed spending time with her and her family, like in the old days, and I realize we still have a lot in common, especially ambition. Maybe that is what also keeps us apart, for now at least. Maybe there will still be a chance for us to have a deeper relationship down the road.

"I always knew you would make it in the big world; you brought us chicken from KFC, even when you were paying rent at the Y and helping your own family out. Mama always liked the way you respected the women folks."

I hug Trudy and say, "Thanks for having me over, and don't sell yourself short. Now that I look back, I understand how much you helped me, and I wonder whether I would have finished high school if it hadn't been for you. I know I wouldn't have had a clue how to study for the university classes if it hadn't been for the way you helped me study. Tell your family and your best buddy Betty hello."

I walk back to the motel a little slower than I walked to Trudy's. An afternoon chill has pushed the porch sitters back inside, so the walk is also quieter. After four days of visiting friends and family, I'm ready to spend a quiet evening and stay home where I can write in my journal and dip back into *War and Peace*.

Trudy's mama is really proud of her, and so am I. I got more respect from Trudy and her mother in two minutes than I ever did at the KFC. All those guys care about is making themselves sound tough and like they are irresistible to women. With Trudy, I could talk about ideas and books and what is important. I feel a little sad that I wasted time listening to guys acting like jerks at a low-paying job and ignored someone who cared about me. It felt good talking about goals with her and finding out that she wants to go to college. Even though we are going our separate ways, we are both looking ahead. I can hold on to that vision and take the beauty of finding a kindred spirit to blaze a way forward.

43

SAYING GOODBYE

NEW YEAR'S DAY, 1970

Arthur and me sit in a booth at the Busy Bee Cafe, each holding a mug of fresh coffee. Arthur talks about New Year's Eve.

"Junebug, you should've come over. We had a feast! Marie's folks brought over a side of pork. She made hushpuppies, and the neighbors brought pie."

"Thanks, Arthur. I can see I missed out, but I had a good New Year's Eve lying low, watching CBS, and watching the ball drop in Times Square. Also, I got to talk to all the folks in Seattle and Detroit. They're all doing well, and I got packed and ready to head home."

Arthur shakes his head doubtfully. "I don't know why you booked a flight on New Year's Day. How are you gonna get a good start on the year without your black-eyed peas? You won't have the money to come back here if you don't eat your greens on New Year's Day."

"I'll eat my parsley," I say, grinning.

Arthur shakes his head, nonplussed.

Our breakfasts arrive, and I want to enjoy my last bowl of Southern grits. Even though Daddy's sisters grew up eating them, they don't much bother cooking them now that they live up north.

Arthur works part time for the church as a handyman and needs to make some rounds. I'm happy to fill the time by going along. We drive away from the city and head out on Highway 61 toward Redwood, where his family has attended church since he was a boy. I'd forgotten the church was so small. Compared to FAME in Seattle, this little church looks insignificant. But remembering the kindness of the church ladies when Mama passed, I smile. I remember how I'd gone to church beside Mama and how gently she'd guide me to sit still and listen to the sermon.

"You know, Arthur," I say, "this little church packs a big punch. I'll bet those old beams are still vibrating from all the hymns sung, sermons preached, and 'amens'."

Arthur nods. "The Church is people coming together to support one another and praise the Lord. The size of the building doesn't matter."

Once there, Arthur sets out about his business, making sure everything is in order for Sunday's service, and I walk over to visit my Mama's grave.

Her marker is small. I pull out the grass crowding around the edges and brush off the slab so I can read the inscription:

1936–1964
Willie B. Reed
Beloved Wife, Daughter
and Mother

I have some news for her and want to find the right words. I empty my thoughts and look inside my memories for her smile. Then I tell her what's on my mind.

Mama, you trusted me and had faith that I could step into Daddy's shoes. I felt like a selfish failure because I couldn't do what I thought the man of the house should do. Now, I'm here to tell you that you did the best you could for us, and so did Daddy, and so did I. One time, I thought the best thing I could do was to bring home chicken from my job, but now I'm learning how it's love that makes us rise—and blame that pulls us down. Because you, Mama Sallie, Mama Lankie, and all the rest of my aunts taught me about the importance of love and family, I had to come back to Redwood to visit my friends and family and talk to you one more time. Now I'm ready to go back to Seattle and focus on school. I'm ready to move past Jim Crow and my anger at Daddy. Maybe someday I'll have a son who doesn't have to live under the rules we knew. You taught me about the importance of love, kindness, and hard work. That's all I need to move on and stay in school.

ACKNOWLEDGMENTS

I want to thank the many people who have helped me bring this book to fruition. I don't want to leave anyone out, but I am sure I have neglected mentioning someone who has been an inspiration along the way, so thanks for your support.

First, my family: Daddy, Wilson Reed Sr., instructed me to put a book under my pillow at night, to do well on my exams. I learned I needed to also read and study, but I knew he was always well intentioned. Gail Ware, my sister, is still with me and keeps me humble with the story that I left her up in a tree for two hours and came back laughing at her for crying. My son, Creighton, who taught me about fatherhood and helped me to understand my own father. My last remaining auntie from Redwood Mississippi, Sally Williams, who was also one of the women who nurtured me in Seattle, passed away in July 2022. She taught me the importance of family relationships, was an educator in the Seattle public schools, and a kindred spirit. I have fond memories of my cousin, Eric Williams, a great guy, and a welcoming sight at the Seattle Public Library.

Second, the road from earning my high school diploma from Rosa A. Temple High School in Vicksburg, Mississippi, to earning my PhD from Northern Arizona University was a long one. Along the way, I received support that helped me navigate the forks in the road. Dr. Dale Edward Wiggins and his wife, Dr. Ruby Wiggins, both fellow graduates from Temple, inspired me at a distance with their dedication to complete the academic journey. K. Scott Christiansen, a dedicated, inspirational educator, who I met while working on a master's degree at SUNY/Albany, New York, encouraged me to take pride in my writing and in my Mississippi heritage. Dr. David Camacho, a professor at Northern Arizona University, enthusiastically supported my aspirations to complete my doctoral degree and advocated for a scholarship and employment in the Criminal Justice department. He was a member of my dissertation committee who inspired and encouraged me through the entire process of earning my doctorate. Dr. Herman Gray has been a friend since my first professional job at Washington State University. He was a solid example of how to be a scholar and educator. Crosbia Anderson, who I also met at WSU while teaching in the African American Studies program, provided me with the mantra to keep working, by continually asking, "Have you finished that book yet?"

I am also grateful to the many friends who have stood by me along the way. Sherri and Ray Williams, Will Witt, Ed Werner, Eugene and Lisa Brown, Rick Reynolds, Harold Bradford, and Bob Ray Sanders—thank you for your enduring friendship.

Third, there are many who have helped to give the little guy who waited for the old school bus in Redwood, Mississippi, a voice. I thank the Ridgecrest Elementary School family for their support and encouragement. The dean of students, Nathan Christian, read *Junebug* and shared it with the staff. Many teachers invited me into their classrooms to share my experiences and stories from the book. Their enthusiasm encouraged me to keep a positive outlook while working through the process of submitting *Junebug* to publishers.

Finally, I thank those who helped bring *Junebug* to the world. First, I thank Matt Lindstrom, professor at St. John's University/St. Benedict College, and my friend. We first met at Northern Arizona University in Flagstaff while working on our doctorates in the early '90s. He was integral to my beginning this project. Several years after our time at N.A.U., he invited me to lecture at St. John's University and St. Benedict College in Minnesota. When the students had more questions about my personal history, my cultural heritage, and how I escaped Mississippi, I realized *Junebug* was a story I needed to write. Dr. Lindstrom contributed to the project both financially and with his enthusiasm, helping me to study the crafts of memoir and fiction writing to bring *Junebug* to the page.

The team at Kevin Anderson and Associates, specifically Julie Watts, was instrumental in transforming my early notes and drafts into a solid story. I also thank the team at the publisher, Morgan James Publishing house. Cortney Donelson formatted and edited my manuscript into a book. I also thank my partner, Toni Harvey for her help in shaping my stories and in developing scenes and dialogue that bring my family and friends to life.

ABOUT THE AUTHOR

Wilson Edward Reed, PhD was born on a family farm in 1950s Mississippi, during the height of Jim Crow segregation. As an African American, he lived under the twenty-two laws that restricted miscegenation (racial mixing) and prevented African Americans from participating as full citizens—for over seventy-five years.

Dr. Reed learned at an early age that he must obey Jim Crow or face punishment. He attended a segregated school, church, movie theater, and public library, and was able to maintain his dignity by working hard in school and taking small jobs, including picking cotton. After attending Rosa A. Temple High School and Utica Junior College, Wilson Reed moved to Seattle and earned both BA and MA degrees at the University of Washington.

Years later, he earned an MA at Suny Albany and finally capped off his academic achievements with a PhD at Northern Arizona in Flagstaff, Arizona. He taught at over five institutions, including the University of Washington, University of Oregon, Seattle University, Northern Arizona University, and Texas Christian University, over his professional career.

Today, Dr. Reed lives outside of Las Vegas, Nevada. His first book, *The Politics of Community Policing* is still in print. This, his newest release, *Junebug,* is a fictionalized account of growing up Black in the South during the 1950s and '60s under Jim Crow.

He is still known affectionately to family and friends from Mississippi as "Junebug." Most of the story is true, and most of the characters are based on real people. He was born in rural Mississippi on a family-owned farm where he worked in the field picking cotton and pulling corn at an early age. The Jim Crow laws did curtail the boundaries of his and his family's life in rural Mississippi. While finding limited opportunities in Mississippi, he blossomed in Seattle. After the bus trip west, the family and community support gave him the confidence and security to grow.

The Sankofa bird is an important symbol of African culture. It signifies the importance of understanding the past to move forward. Dr. Reed never forgot his humble beginnings. Throughout his career, he's worked to highlight the problems that divide communities and to bring students toward an understanding of ways to appreciate our differences.

A free ebook edition is available with the purchase of this book.

To claim your free ebook edition:

1. Visit MorganJamesBOGO.com
2. Sign your name CLEARLY in the space
3. Complete the form and submit a photo of the entire copyright page
4. You or your friend can download the ebook to your preferred device

Morgan James
BOGO™

A **FREE** ebook edition is available for you or a friend with the purchase of this print book.

CLEARLY SIGN YOUR NAME ABOVE

Instructions to claim your free ebook edition:
1. Visit MorganJamesBOGO.com
2. Sign your name CLEARLY in the space above
3. Complete the form and submit a photo of this entire page
4. You or your friend can download the ebook to your preferred device

Print & Digital Together Forever.

Snap a photo

Free ebook

Read anywhere

Printed in the USA
CPSIA information can be obtained
at www.ICGtesting.com
JSHW021351191223
54035JS00002B/84